WAL... ...S DOG
AND O... ...ER SHORT STORIES

STEVE CHILTON

TAKAHE PUBLISHING LTD
2016

This edition published 2016 by

Takahe Publishing Ltd.
Registered Office:
77 Earlsdon Street, Coventry CV5 6EL

Copyright ©Steve Chilton 2016

ISBN 978-1-908837-07-3

The moral rights of the author have been asserted

All rights reserved. This publication may not be reproduced, stored in a retrieval system or transmitted, in any form or by any means, electronic, mechanical, photocopying, recording or otherwise, without the prior permission of the publishers.

Permissions and references:

RIDERS ON THE STORM
Words and Music by The Doors
Copyright 1971 (renewed) Doors Music Co.
Exclusive worldwide print rights administered by ALFRED MUSIC
All rights reserved. Used by permission.

The author gratefully acknowledges the following publications as sources of background information.
Life, by Keith Richards with James Fox.
The Rolling Stones On Tour:Report and Interview by Robert Greenfield, Rolling Stone, April 1971.
Secrets of the Flesh, A Life of Colette, by Judith Thurman

This book is a work of fiction and except in the case of historical fact (see author's notes, page 221) any resemblance to actual persons living or dead, is purely coincidental.

For Finch, on completion of her apprenticeship in forbearance.

Contents

Page 1 Walking Keef's Dog
Keef arrives for a gig clutching neither his gorgeous girlfriend nor other stimulants, but his cute puppy, Boogie, whose escape sparks a canine romp of sex, drugs and rock 'n stroll.

Page 23 La Mer
Reynard Blythe's career of drudgery changes key when he takes up the squeezebox and pursues his dream in the south of France.

Page 37 Pinky and Perky
A drug to perk up giant pandas is a hit with fans at folk festivals but Inspector Theo Monk is on the trail of the gang pulling the strings.

Page 73 She's a Killer... Queen
A romantic picnic leads to slaughter at a village wedding and a startling confession by Queen Elizabeth.

Page 89 The Ballad of Jim and Oscar
Waking the dead at Père Lachaise cemetery, Paris, where feuding residents Oscar Wilde and Jim Morrison rise to the occasion when challenged to put up or shut up.

Page 123   The Boys are back in town
A coroner's court hears that foul play by a beef burger may have caused a football fan to pay the ultimate penalty for behaving badly.

Page 147   You Better, You Bet!
A new hospital is keeping a bizarre fund-raising scheme under wraps but all is revealed during a wheelchair time trial on the wards.

Page 161   Oh, No, Not Romeo
Wherefore art thou, Antonio? Up in the gallery, moonlighting as a music hall star. There he is, can't you see?

Page 189   White Jacket
Labour warhorse Bill Sheepshank has run his race but still grabs the glory at his own funeral, leaving his rival trailing at the wake.

Page 215   When Blue turns to Grey
A national treasure tries to emulate 50 Shades with a bonkbuster for oldies; the plan collapses when his paste-table does the same under the weight of his home help.

1.
Walking Keef's Dog

THIS must've been what it was like after Keef fell from that tree in Fiji.

Brain teetering on the axis of bliss and oblivion, cocooned in a muffle of distorted ambient sound. Pondering why a right leg that is close enough to be mine is pointing at the ceiling. Shapes emerge through the drug-sweetened fug and slowly focus until a bare big toe peeps at me from a sheath of white plaster.

The blancmange of noise is breaking into separate dollops. Yapyapyap... weasel voice...yap yap... no nonsense voice... yap...doors banging...muted yap... scuffles.

'Get. Yourself. And. That. Dog. Out of here right now or I'll call hospital security,' barks no nonsense.

'Sister, please,' weasel voice begs, 'the readers of the Telegraph are crying out for news of a local hero, and we'll be sure to mention the wonderful care he's receiving here. It'll be great publicity for you. Just one

picture of this pup and the patient and we'll be gone…'
The answer comes in a screech of leather soles being dragged across hard lino to an acapella of doggy yelps and banging bed pans. It sends me back down the spinning rabbit hole to the safety of dreams.

Dead Flowers

Most things had bypassed Coventry by the second half of the Sixties. Even the M1 went out of its way to sneak past. The Summer of Love, if it ever happened, didn't surface here. Sons of car workers wouldn't have minded a shot at free love and Columbian Gold but drew the line at kaftans and cowbells.

We made do with Embassy Regal and hummed along to *Are You Going to San Francisco?* as Pan's People pranced about with flowers in their hair in a Shepherd's Bush Studio.

Fashion failed to find the momentum to swing 90 miles north of the King's Road to Coventry. The Mod rebels lost their cause as the Sixties dispersed into myth, let their hair grow and swapped vented suits for scuffed leather and stonewash denim. Others mutated into skinhead/suedeheads. Razored their hair, grew real sideburns, and turned up their Levis above red-laced Doc Martens. Ugly, aggressive and unloved. A perfect fit for a brutally dysfunctional city centre.

Hitler's bombers shouldered most of the blame for that. By not bypassing Coventry 25 years earlier. The Blitz took out most of the old centre and left civic planners with a blank canvas, which they eagerly filled in with a cubist orgy of grey concrete.

But the Luftwaffe hadn't got it all. The Coventry Theatre, an art deco monolith from the age of variety hall, had stood solid as a rock, immune from the incendiaries that razed the nearby cathedral.

The Stones didn't bypass unfashionable Cov either. They first arrived at the theatre in 1964 on the tail of Beatlemania. Jagger dressed down in those days, nothing fancier than a grey crew neck or a hooped t-shirt. Now, on March 6, 1971, they were back with Jagger suited by Mr Fish in dogtooth check. Accessorised with an impossibly exotic girlfriend, Bianca Pérez Mora Macias.

It's the third date on the so-called 'Farewell Tour' before departing to record *Exile on Main Street*. In reality, exile in the South of France from the UK taxman's demands of 90 percent of their earnings. But no matter. Jagger is still Jumpin' Jack Flash to those of us raised on tribal allegiances. Mick, the butterfly unbroken on a wheel, naked girl in sheepskin rug Jagger.

'Stones or Beatles, mate?'

'Knob off. I'm slashing up the garage wall. Go and hold your bird's hand, Moptop.'

And here they are outside the Coventry Theatre, rolling out of limos parked up along a cobbled lane (another bit Hitler missed) by the stage door.

I'm here. Watching.

How could anyone not be? Didn't they need to know if Jagger was tall and sinewy, as he appeared on TV, or a scrawny short arse, as his bitchy interviewers claimed? Or to see Wyman with his dodgy Cavalier's barnet stride in stone-faced, holding his bass guitar erect, like on stage?

Charlie Watts, the great enigma. Chiselled looks of a Hollywood Sioux brave but shops in Savile Row. What's the betting he'll have on a rakish neckerchief, a reminder to himself he's in a rock and roll band not a jazz quartet?

And Keith? Shit, which could miss seeing the Stones' true bad boy in the flesh? The Artful Dodger to Jagger's grammar school Oliver. It could be his last appearance on earth, let alone in Coventry, if half the rumours of his drug intake are right.

Keith will tumble out of a Roller in a cascade of syringes and empty whisky bottles. For sure. Only question is, will it be a half dressed, ravishingly decadent Anita Pallenberg hitting the pavement with him or his other partner in excess, soulmate Gram Parsons? Probably both. It was neither.

Bitch

Keith steps out the car that's taxied him from Coventry railway station clutching Boogie, a cute brown and white King Charles spaniel pup. The sort of accessory usually only favoured by blokes as chatup bait for gullible women, blind to the wolf holding it. But not rock stars, for Christ's sake. Least of all Keith Richards. Bloody hell.

Despite being held protectively, saucer- eyed Boogie is fretful. She needs to follow in her owner's infamous footsteps and pee up the nearest wall. A front paw is tucked securely inside Keith's belt buckle but it doesn't prevent her fidgeting. The persistent blinking is a result of being downwind of two minders chatting outside the stage door. Pungent herbal smoke is making its way up her snub nose.

All the Stones are behind a police cordon that seals off the lane from the main road and the fans. Not that there's a massive turnout. The screaming hysteria that marked the '64 visit has time-lapsed, the ritual passed down to younger sisters in waiting for their own idols. There's a few, though, turning back the years, waving bits of paper for autographs. But the mood is sombre. The gathering, like a herd of feral grazers, feels a tremor, sniffs more than weed on the breeze.

The Stones' fault line was starting to show even in this shabby lane. Jagger seems to be ignoring Keith and the dog. Bianca, draped in a huge linen cloak and sporting a floppy cowboy hat the size of parasol, looks dressed for Ladies' Day at a Summer Solstice. She is ignoring everyone.

If the tabloids are right, she's two months pregnant. She radiates indifference, seemingly unaware that she is in the eye of a storm. Jagger is making sure the photographers can't get a closeup of them together and stays a few paces ahead with a scowling Charlie Watts, disappointingly wearing neither a Savile Row suit nor a neckerchief.

Is Keith deliberately upstaging Jagger even before the concert starts? Rock's greatest frontman has brought along one of the world's most beautiful women to the gig. His old mucker from Dartford, 'Keef,' has turned up with a dog. And he is lapping it up, posing for the cameras, smiling and looking happy as Boogie wriggles and yaps.

And then it kicks off.

A tempest in the form of an unwanted groupie breaks through the police cordon yelling, 'You bastards...you fucking bastard Stones' and makes a beeline for Jagger. A burly minder launches himself at her, misses and instead propels Jagger, whose arm is poised for a hand-off, clattering into Keith and Boogie.

The spaniel's bog eyes, now entirely black due to the pupil-dilating effects of passive pot sniffing, collide like vinyl 45s on wonky turntables. Eyes unable to reflect her terror, Boogie's tiny brain alerts an alternative outlet and a jet of warm puppy pee hits Keith's stomach.

He buckles as if hit by a low blow, throws his arms in the air, launching Boogie into a backward somersault, trailing an arc of canine piss. It forms momentarily like an avenging rainbow over Jagger's sprawled body, then sprinkles down on his famous tousled locks and designer suit.

'Bitch, stupid bloody bitch,' Jagger curses, swinging out a flared leg in fury, but Boogie is already disappearing under a forest of police legs and press photographers. The next day's tabloids would report the melee under variations of the headline 'Street Fighting Men' with a picture of Jagger, Richards, groupie and minder in an ungainly tangle on the cobbles.

I wasn't around to see it. A familiar voice was screaming at me 'Grab the dog, get the dog...stop it!' It was mine. Urging me on as I belted round the corner, barging a path through the now-animated fans and befuddled coppers, in pursuit of Boogie. But the dog had gone, vanished into thin air.

Paint it Black

Jagger is in his cups in the theatre restaurant, brooding over an inedible burger and the first house audience. Both have an equal share of his contempt. For the first time on the tour he's failed to get the fans on their feet, let alone dancing in the aisles. Finally, they are stirred from the seats when their stage manager decides to end the misery with a recording of the National Anthem. He was taking the piss but it worked. They stood, they whistled and cheered and filed out like a Last Night of The Proms' crowd. Probably not as raucous. Jagger didn't see the funny side, though. It should have ended on an encore of *Sympathy for the Devil* with him throwing daffodils into the audience.

'What's the matter with them?' he asks Bianca, who shows her concern by carrying on playing with a yoyo and not answering.

'You know what, I don't fucking care. If the next lot are the same we'll chop the encore again. Who cares?' he adds rhetorically.

Charlie and Keith exchange a knowing glance. Is he talking about the gig or the group? Is his heart in the Stones anymore? Bianca has been a game changer, moves in a society whirl of loaded Euro aristos and movie stars, clearly not cut from rockchick material. Her natural habitats are the fashion houses of Paris. Within two months she will marry Mick in St Tropez, Roger Vadim as best man. The roots of Jagger's socialite tendency are ready to be nourished by the Paris glitterati.

The threat that poses to the band may be the underlying cause of the bad blood. This time it's seeped through to into the engine room of the band: Keith and Charlie, the dynamo that powered them from the Crawdaddy in Richmond to the world stage. Watts turns the key, Richards puts his foot on the gas. From the first note, the audience knows where it's heading and is in the passenger seat waiting for Jagger.

'C'mon Mick, you met a gin-soaked bar-room queen in Memphis...'

But something hadn't been right at the first house. A matinee, for a start. No place for a nocturnal rock band. Daylight exposure does little to help transport the fans to a world of honky tonk women in the Deep South when they've just stepped off a bus in grey Coventry. The show stuttered from the opening bars of *Jumpin' Jack Flash* through to the premature closer, *Street Fightin' Man*. By the Stones' standards it was down there with the puddle left behind by Boogie. Piss Poor.

Outside the theatre restaurant, the Stones' road man-

Walking Keef's Dog

ager and a two-man film crew are in crisis talks. The matinee footage had already been consigned to the bin. Hopes that Coventry would provide a hefty chunk of the tour documentary now rested on the second house performance. Brave faces fooled no one.

The producer is masking his delight over the cranked up tension between the two main players. But he's worried that'll overshadow the performances of a band billed as the greatest on the planet.

'Judging by what we've just seen,' he quips to the cameraman, 'that planet is Mars. No bloody atmosphere.'

If anything was to be salvaged, the second house would have to be a hell of a lot better. That'd only happen if they could somehow snap Keith from his malaise over losing Boogie. A pep talk and a glass of Jack Daniels to the maestro of the artificial quick fix? It'd be like offering a below par Hendrix a new plectrum and telling him to buck his ideas up. Better to take a few shots themselves and hope for a blinding flash of inspiration.

Desperation however proves the mother of invention. 'Get a cute dog,' the tour manager suddenly barks at the bruised bodyguard who'd thrown himself at the groupie.

'Long as it looks something like a fucking spaniel, brown and white, a little bastard, it'll do. Keith won't know the difference; his eyes are bigger than the dog's by now. Besides you'll be standing halfway up the stalls holding it up and we'll have that spotlight on and off you before you can say ringer.'

With that, a handful of blue fivers are thrust into the

dumbstruck minder's fat fist with the parting command: 'There's pet shop over the road in the shopping precinct, start there. If they ain't got one, get yourself down the nearest dogs' home.

'I don't care if you come back with a sodding big guinea pig with floppy ears. It doesn't have to act. Now piss off. You've got an hour.'

The producer hides a smirk with a forced cough. It's a win-win. If Keef falls for it, which is highly unlikely, it will lift the mood, at least for the show. But when, not if, he rumbles the deception... well, the eruption should give him the blistering farewell film all right. Goodbye Forever, Greatest Band on the Planet.

Tumbling Dice

Time wasn't on my side. How the bloody hell could a frightened pup disappear in a city centre imprisoned by a ring road? There was no way the little bugger could cross without ending up a brown and white shagpile carpet embedded in tarmac.

I was sure Boogie would dodge into Lady Herbert's Garden, a small park at the back of the theatre, named after the wife of an Edwardian factory owner and benefactor. Now a winos' haunt.

Spaniels are the dog world's flushers, right? Bred to duck and dive into hedgerows, rooting out anything hiding in there to provide a moving target for trigger happy toffs.

Walking Keef's Dog

The park was an instinctive home for a stampeding spaniel, it had more nooks and crannies than a junkies' squat. A 100-yard strip on both sides provided a defiant tangle of neglected grasses, weeds, strangled shrubs and thorny bushes. They're a formidable barrier around a decaying red brick pavilion with broken cellar windows at dog height. Clumps of densely planted acers and willows weep down at the shabby lawns, as voluminous as Bianca's cape.

After an hour of searching I am ready to give it up and get back to the theatre for the second show. I'd queued for an entire morning for my seat in the circle and if I don't get back pronto it'll be the only empty one in the theatre.

I was so sure of finding Boogie I'd moved on in my mind to savour my rewards. An emotional Keef (as he'd insist I call him) would be so grateful he'd invite me to the Stones' aftershow party; we'd bitch about Chuck Berry while praising his artistry, fend off a dozen groupies and sink a bottle of Jack Daniels, probably two. I'd move into his gaff at Cheyne Walk, hang out with him Anita, Gram and Boogie. I'd probably agree to take Boogie over to the South of France after quarantine, sit in on Exile recording sessions....

'Oi, you!' The challenge comes from a fireman at the gate, breaking the spell. 'What's going on?'

'Not a fire, obviously,' I'm tempted to yell back. The old fire station is closing after 60 years and a new one is being built around the corner. Only one crew remains. In between 'Shouts' they spend the day polishing the sole fire engine, kicking a ball about or lobbing it at a basketball ring in the yard.

'I'm looking for a dog, a little spaniel.'

'Sure you are, probably with your flies undone you little pervert. Bugger off before I have you arrested.'

In rapid fire gasps I tell him the story of Keith's runaway and his face starts to lose its official mask, nearly breaks into a grin.

'So that's what the freaks were up to,' he says.

'Coventry's lost tribe of hippies, four of 'em were in here earlier, smoking dope again. Gives our young cadets something to spot from the lookout tower.

'Then one of us'll come over and threaten to set the hose on their little party.

'Instead of calling me a pig, as they usually do, this time they shoved something that looked like a bed roll in a tote bag and shuffled out. Went off towards the Swanswell.'

He'd barely finished the last word and I was haring off up Primrose Hill to a scruffy man-made lake, bordered by concrete, naturally, where inner city swans slummed, dreaming of a better life on the Avon at Stratford.

Even if I'd been blind I would've pinned the hippies down within a foot of entering the park. A waft of marijuana steered my nose to the abductors grouped in a tight circle, crossed-legged, by the water's edge. In the centre, a zonked out brown and white dog more stoned than them.

No time for reason, no point in it either judging from the blank stares from five pairs of eyes. Speak to them in their native tongue.

'Split man, the pigs are on to you. They know you've kidnapped the dog... you're gonna get busted,' I scream.

A hairy quartet of Afghan coats rise as one like a spooked eight-legged yak and bolts for the far gate without a backward glance to its abandoned trophy, pausing only to lob a cigar-sized joint to the swill of the lake, narrowly missing an upturned duck

Satisfaction

The dream is back on. Grabbing Boogie by her collarless ruff, I spin back towards the theatre, prising her slobbering mouth open to take in the headwind. False bravado gives me an adrenaline boost and inside four minutes rejuvenated legs deliver us to the stagedoor, which is being battered by my free fist. The second show should be just beginning. Jagger swirling to *Jumping Jack Flash*, dazzling in the pink satin baseball outfit he'd concocted. I'm Jumpin' Jack Flash. It's a gas.

'Let me in, I've got the dog.' Bash! Bash! Bash!

Amazingly the door opens a few inches and the wary nose of stagedoor old retainer Sid appears, his beady eyes oddly welcoming.

'You took your time, didn't you? The show's started. They said you'd be coming in the front so you could get down the aisle. Bloody daft idea if you want my opinion. I'll give you this though, the dog's a bloody good match for the little sod that ran off. Follow me, we'll go through the back of the stage. You'll have to stand behind the curtain. Keep the bugger quiet or you'll give the game away.'

At that, Boogie's eyes spark into life and she lunges at Sid's beaky nose, missing the tip by a whisker but leaving a sliver of saliva across his wrinkled cheek.

The reaction diverts me from asking the old curmudgeon, who lives by the mantra They shall Not Pass, what the hell he's prattling on about.

'No time to get you out front, you'll have to stand in the wings,' Sid continues, wiping away the slobber.

As we make our way through the darkness backstage the noise is deafening. Jagger is back to full pomp and the fans are going crazy. The first six rows have abandoned seats and are pressed up against the orchestra pit baying for him to come to them. Those who try to scramble over the pit barrier face a six-foot drop and a moat of grim-faced heavies ready to hurl them back again. Above them a group of headbangers are hanging out a balcony box like manic puppets, arms flailing, and hair cascading, matching Jagger pout for pout.

Jagger turns and faces the rest of the Stones, nods to Charlie and stops singing. The rhythm is suddenly on tick over; the bewildered fans take up the chorus thinking they're being shortchanged: *Jumpin Jack Flash, it's a gas...Jumping Jack Flash... it's a gas.*

Jagger turns back to the stand mic, flapping his arms in a plea for quiet. Charlie is marking time. Bill and Mick Taylor fall in. Only Keith looks baffled and throws in one last lick, looks daggers at Jagger and strums.

Walking Keef's Dog

Hands on hips, Jagger is at his most camp. He stares directly at the audience and affects his best mockney. Letting them in on a confidence. 'Well you're a bloody improvement on the last bunch of miserable fuckers that were in 'ere,' he says. Charlie pings the cymbal to underline Mick's 'aving a larf.

'Keef's brought a lot of dogs to our gigs,' Jagger shouts, arms akimbo and hips thrust forward just in case anyone missed the innuendo.

'But today is the first time one's fucked off before the party's started.'

The lusty laugh of the 2,000 audience makes him oblivious to Keef's eyes burning a hole in the back of his baseball jacket. He's into his stride.

'No, honestly, the bitch took off like she'd got a rocket up her arse. Left him just like that, one of his favourites too. You'd think he'd be used to it by now.'

A dull thump from Charlie's bass drum warns him that he's in imminent danger of having a rhythm guitar wrapped around his neck. A darting backwards glance confirms the alert. Bobby Keys has his sax pressed against Keef's chest but is losing the fight to keep him back.

'Don't get the wrong idea, now,' implores Jagger unconvincingly. 'It was Keef's pet dog, Boogie, that buggered off, probably trying to find a patch of grass in all this concrete you got here.'

The audience gives a halfhearted cheer, not sure now who Jagger is having a laugh at. He throws them a bone.

'Not as bad as Birmingham, though,' he says and is

rewarded by more raucous cheers.

'But, listen up. I've got some good news for Keef.'

It's the cue for a spotlight to swing across the audience and stop above two figures in shadow halfway up the left hand aisle. The beam drops dramatically, illuminating a red-faced bouncer struggling to hold on to a spaniel. A black and white Springer.

'We've found Boogie for Keef!' shouts Jagger triumphantly as Charlie smashes his cymbals in acclaim. The audience starts chanting "Boogie...Boogie-Boogie..."

The euphoria is contagious, but it's not gripped Keef. He's apoplectic, and is swinging his guitar like an axe.

'That's not my Boogie you twats,' he roars, and trips over a cable as he launches a strike to decapitate the singer.

Fate had decreed that this would be the precise moment that real Boogie and I emerge from the backstage blackness, guided by Sid's torch.

Boogie, fired up by the sound of her master's voice, is straining every sinew to get to him and is in danger of being throttled by my trouser belt. It was pressed into action as a makeshift lead but is tightening like a noose, and I'm the hangman. I ease my grip, cutting her a bit of slack. In a flash Boogie grabs the advantage and surges forward for her stage debut. My instinctive yank back is too late.

Boogie bounds onto the boards with unbridled joy. I'm a belt-length behind holding on with one hand and to my dignity with the other as my trousers start to descend. Already drunk on the unfolding mayhem, the audience ramps up the crescendo to a baying wall of sound, pierced only by soaring lead vocals of the headbangers who are conducting the upper balcony in a chorus of "there's only two boogie woogies...two boogie woogies..."

Jagger's executing an impressive onelegged backslide, pinched from James Brown, which has taken him clear of the decapitation zone. Keith is up on his feet again and hugging Boogie like a returning mistress.

The devil in Jagger shows no sympathy and spots potential for more baiting. 'Bloody hell,' he shouts across the audience cheers, 'we've got two fucking Boogies, now. Will the real one please step forward?'

Keith isn't letting go and I'm rigid with stage fright, trapped in the glare of the spotlight that has switched from Bogus Boogie and his minder. Jagger scurries around the rest of the Stones shouting instructions I can't make out, while raising clapping hands to exhort more applause.

And he gets it. Completing his circle around the stage, he grabs Keef by the shoulders, plants a kiss on his cheek, whispers conspiratorially in his ear and gives Boogie's coat an affectionate ruffle. I get just a nod and Jagger points me to the side of the stage like a naughty schoolboy. I'm about to slope off in disgrace when he winks and hands me the lead.

'Stand there with the dog and wait for your cue. Just follow me, all right?'

Walking the Dog

'Boogie's back, been off track, left Keef on the rack,' Jagger hollers into the mic to the opening bars of the Rufus Thomas's classic *Walking the Dog*.

It's a song the band cut its teeth on scratching a living in the pubs and clubs of London. The audience knows it just as well and lets out a huge roar. It could have drowned out the next line, but Jagger's pausing for effect.

Keith is beaming, eyes fully on Jagger, ears tuned to Charlie's drums, already mouthing the next line. Jagger milks the suspense, waits for another beat and let's fly.

The audience joins him in a raucous invitation to get on tippy toes and learn how to walk the dog. No-one cares whether it's a dance or, more likely, something more earthy. Tonight it gets the benefit of the doubt and is being taken literally.

With his intimidating blank stare, Jagger struts towards me, chest out like a rooster, thumbs resting behind silk lapels. Boogie is ready to bolt again.

I know exactly what's coming. Jagger forms a circle with his thumb and index finger, shoves it between his pumped up lips and emits three impressive dog whistles as Keith shouts the chorus, *C'mon C'mon C'mon...*

Jagger spins as he reaches us and sashays away to the beat. We follow. I'm entranced, strutting across the apron of the stage, pulling a hesitant Boogie. But she's getting no mercy this time from the noose. The message is clear: Move your ass, Missy. Showtime.

Walking Keef's Dog

I've gone from stage mouse to stage lion in a few steps, wallowing in the applause. A Stone, gladiator to groupies, Jagger's apprentice, lust icon to deliriously rampant girls.

And totally oblivious to his instruction to leave the stage after the first pass. Jagger's back at the stand mic preparing to repossess the limelight as I turn at the curtain, drawn back by fame's magnet; the smell of the crowd, the roar of my ego.

'Hi ho from tip to toe, come on Boogie here we go,' I shout down at my co-star.

By the time Jagger's realised I'd rebelled, we were on the unscheduled return. We reach halfway across the line of footlights and I see Jagger's petulant pout and decide to retaliate, turn to face the audience, pout my lips and thrust out my hip in imitation.

It brings the house down. But it also brings the red mist down on Bogus Boogie who's been left unguarded since the spotlight shifted off him. Jealousy or lust - for it was soon all too apparent he was a dog – gets the better of him seeing a bitch parading within striking distance. He bounds towards us, clearing the steps to the stage in one mighty leap, howling like a wolf. Real Boogie circles me in terror, looping the makeshift lead around my ankles with a force strong enough to send me tottering.

Headlong into the orchestra pit.

In years to come the technique would be developed into crowdsurfing, with one obvious improvement. My pilot dive leaves me an orchestra pit-width short of the fans. I land on something human but unbending, later identified as a flattened bouncer. Boogie is wound around my left leg by a belt, her mouth clamped to my ankle. Bogus Boogie is furiously humping my other leg which sticks out at right angles from the rest of me.

Few hear my scream for the thunderous clapping and cheering as Jagger ad libs: 'If you dunno how to do it, don't try to dance like me...'

It's All Over Now

'Come on sweetheart, wake up. It's time for your drugs and a bath.'

An angel is hovering over me. I can just make out the name Anita on a brilliant luminescent tunic. Christ, I've died and gone to Stones' heaven: Anita Pallenberg is about to join me in a bath and spoon feed me happy pills. It's a remake of 'Performance' and I've been handed Jagger's role.

'Did I see you down in San Antone on a hot and dusty night...?' I burble in a pathetic attempt to show her I can sing Memo to Turner before she runs the hot tap.

'I don't think so, Love. Is it in Spain?' she says in that over-friendly way that nurses affect to cover up not remembering your name.

'You've had a little accident, darling. Been with us in hospital for two days now; the painkillers have made you a bit dopey.'

'A big dopey?' I groan to myself as the true picture of what's happened dawns.

Walking Keef's Dog

'Of course not,' says Anita. 'You've become quite a celebrity. We had to chuck out a reporter this morning. Cheeky devil marched in here with a big dog asking if we would mind his photographer taking a snap of it on the bed next to you sleeping.

'And just look at all these cards and flowers you've been sent,' she adds, waving her thermometer at two pots of daffs and a pile of envelopes, theatrically pointing at the largest, and raises a knowing eyebrow. I recognise the rude logo immediately. A big red rasping tongue, the Stones graphic for the new Sticky Fingers album.

'I'll get it for you, er, Pet,' she falters, fast running out of alternatives for my name.

I'd later regret tearing the envelope from both corners. But this was a message from Keef, Mick ... Charlie, the other Mick, Bill ... My Band.

My God.

Jagger had made an effort, of sorts. 'Don't give up the day job, love Mick.'

The other three signatures look suspiciously similar to each other and have a feminine lightness. But I don't give a toss. The cartoon on the back of card has acted like a steamy soak with Anita. A stupid grin is spreading across my face as I stare at the silhouette of a dog's pawprint roughly drawn with eyeliner. Below it the message: 'You DON'T know how to do it, so I'll show you how to walk the friggin' dog when you've recovered

Keef and BoogieX.'

*Author's note: no animals were injured during the making up of this report, although the truth took a hammering. The Stones did indeed appear for two shows in Coventry in March 1971. I was in the audience for the second, to this day the best live performance by a rock band I've seen and ever likely to. Keith did arrive with a pet spaniel called Boogie and it's broadly true that a rift in his well-documented relationship with Jagger was starting to develop. However, the remainder of the story is pure fantasy. Boogie has long gone to the great kennel in the sky; the Coventry Theatre is buried too, entombed beneath a desolate public square. But the greatest band on the planet rolls on. Long may they stay earthbound.

2.
La Mer

THERE was little applause when Reynard Blythe left work for the last time after 45 years' service.

It wasn't that he was unpopular, simply that there were few workmates left to send him off. At 63, he could look back on a job that had been in its death throes from the first day he walked through the gates of the print works.

When he began as an 18-year-old straight from the sixth-form, the days of hot metal in the newspaper industry had already melted away. Compositors were passed reporters' copy typed on small squares of cheap paper, marked brutally by the sub-editor's pencil.

Once reporters were given computers it was obvious to Reynard that the comp's job, in the jargon of the day, was one keystroke too many. Despite that he managed to hold on to a job. Not his old one, of course, that had been consigned to the scrapheap, along with typewriters. Somehow he'd managed to cling on by doing a variety of production jobs with the 'inkies', as the printers were sneeringly called by the journalists, but each one had been picked off by the death-march of technology until he had reached a full stop. The end of his work sentence.

So it was not with a heavy heart that he stood before a handful of colleagues, none of whom he'd known for more than a few years, to receive his leaving present and a few well-meant but meaningless farewell homilies.

'Wish I was joining you, Reynard' . . . 'All that time on your hands, you lucky bastard' . . . ' You're doing the right thing by getting out now . . .'

'Sure,' he thought, as he held on to the box, wrapped thoughtfully in that day's edition of the Herald. 'And you have a nice day, too. I'll just sod off and die now.'

But he didn't give voice to his feelings. He thanked them profusely for the gift. 'Just what he wanted.' That much at least was genuine. He had bought it himself.

His line-manager, whose line was looking increasingly faint, had approached him a week or so earlier with the unease of weasel sent to counsel a fox to inform him that £70 had been collected and 'would he like it in M&S vouchers?'

'I'd prefer Anne Summers, if that's all right,' he told his young boss, relishing the fleeting second of doubt in his eyes before he laughed.

'You nearly had me there, Reynard,' he spluttered.

'I'd like a squeezebox,' Reynard countered.

'Aha, wouldn't we all, you old dog,' said the younger

man, miming a dig in the ribs.

'No, I really would,' said Reynard. 'A concertina, commonly known as a squeezebox. A second-hand English squeezebox. That's what I want.'

Until then, his improbable plan was still a half hidden folder in the section marked Fantasy at the back of his mind. It had taken the realisation that he had been considered an M&S voucher man to drag it from its safe recess and turn thoughts into action.

After a few hours of scouring the internet he had found what he was after. A 48-key chromatic English concertina that had lain unloved and unsqueezed in an attic in a Birmingham semi, once the pride and joy of the householder's grandfather. It had cost him £500, but he wasn't going to tell his workmates that. Their donation would go towards its renovation and tuning. If he did nothing else but hold it and admire the 100-year-old workmanship, the burnished rosewood sides with their leather thumb straps and ivory keys, he would have been content. But only for about an hour.

Although it was a thing of beauty in its own right, he intended to learn to play it well enough to master just one song. One tune that was the essential ingredient in his plan to mark his new life. Maybe the end of it.

Since the death of his wife, he had little enthusiasm for living. He'd led an unexceptional life, dull to the point where his name, Reynard, was the most exceptional thing about him. He had lost count of the number of times people would say to him: 'What an unusual name, where does it come from?' knowing their quizzical pose would turn to a fixed smile when he replied, 'My mother thought I looked like a fox.'

The truth was, although he had entered the world with a thatch of rust-coloured hair, she simply liked the sound of the name. When he was growing up he liked to think it gave him a connection with France, the home of the old tales about Reynard, the wily peasant-hero fox.

He loved the romance of the country even before he stepped foot there. Then he went on a school trip as a 14-year-old across the Channel and was captivated. While the other boys drifted away from the teacher and bought cigarettes and penknives, he wandered the Boulogne streets alone. He didn't want to smoke but he relished the smell of Gauloises drifting across from the street cafes; coveted the yellow and red Ricard ashtrays on the tables, was fascinated by the huge sign-written petrol adverts on gable walls, fading pop-art before the term was coined. He found a playground with swings whose seats of oak were glass-smooth through decades of wear, a roundabout that had carried generations of children, now eroded of paint but turning as sweetly as a freshly-oiled wheel with barely a push. Everything cared for like a cherished elderly relative who was gently slipping away. How different from his own local 'rec' where the equipment had been designed with the expectation it would face an army of vandals. It had the shelf life of a French loaf not a French playground.

And so he had grown up as a closet Francophile, in

love with La Belle France he'd fallen for as a schoolboy. Or, rather, the idea of France. In his imagination he was the adolescent adventurer Le Grand Meaulnes, chasing a dream that would never be realised. And the soundtrack that epitomised his wistful romance was the song La Mer, written and performed by the chanteur Charles Trenet. For Reynard, in no other language could this paean to the sea sound so glorious; no one other than a Frenchman could be so passionate and not sound ridiculous singing it. Reynard knew instinctively that Trenet would not be offering his hymn to the English Channel or La Manche as the French steadfastly called the strip of cold turbulence that so aptly separated the two countries. So it was no surprise when he discovered that the singer had once lived on a cliffside in the most southerly part of France, looking out across the Mediterranean near the border with Spain.

When he reached 60, a year after his wife died, he spent part of his annual summer holiday on a five-day coach tour entitled 'Art and the Catalan region.' The bus driver pointed the Trenet house out flippantly as he drove the hot and largely uninterested passengers along the coast to their hotel destination in Collioure.

'I don't suppose many of you will have heard of Charles Trenet,' the driver said smugly. 'But that's where he used to live up on the cliff-top. He sang La Mer.'

Which was the main reason Reynard had taken the tour. He'd worked out that the route had to take him past Trenet's old home and it was enough to glimpse it fleetingly. He could live on the memory of a brief encounter. Had no wish to visit and find his dream broken by the reality of discovering it had become La Mer Hotel or something worse. Or at least those were his thoughts before reaching the old fishing port of Collioure, announced by the driver, who doubled as the art guide, as 'made famous by the artists Henri Matisse and Andre Derain, the birthplace of fauvism, the wild beast of art.'

Even the hordes of tourists packing the narrow lanes and filling every harbour cafe couldn't dispel Reynard's enchantment with the town. Rather they increased its intensity. As they gawped and clicked, shopped and ate, the noise created an ambient murmur, a counterpoint to the soaring music pounding on his private bubble. The waves were crashing on the base of the church of Notre Dame des Anges as an accordion player played a medley for the tourists filing in dutifully, the odd one pausing to fish out a euro to toss into the instrument's case, which was carefully positioned in the shadow cast by the odd, rather phallic, lighthouse attached to the church.

This was where the idea began which would become his retirement finale; the poke in the eye to those who had him down as an M&S voucher dullard. Reynard started to dream on that blazing July day that he would return to Collioure and play La Mer on the squeezebox. A one-off performance only; for the enjoyment and fulfilment of one. Himself.

And now here he was, moist hands gripping two cases, one guarding the squeezebox, the other containing enough clothing to get him through three days, stepping out from the sweaty heat of a taxi hired at Perpignan airport and checking into the Hotel Matisse in Collioure. He thought he would enjoy the rest of the day strolling by the quayside and wandering around the fortress, once the summer palace of the Kings of Majorca. Perhaps even have a plate of moules and frites before turning in for the night to dream of his dream becoming reality the next day.

The 20-something receptionist eyed his odd-shaped case curiously and then Reynard himself with a flicker of apprehension as he entered the air-conditioned lobby. He had seen this look before, and it usually preceded bad news about a room either not being ready, or worse, it was in an annexe halfway up an adjoining street. His suspicions were increased with the buzz of what sounded like a hundred voices chorusing greetings to one another in the Derain Restaurant off to the side of the lobby where waiters were scurrying to and fro holding trays of wine aloft.

'Bonjour, Monsieur Reynard,' said the receptionist, in a clumsy attempt at friendliness for a reason that would soon become apparent. 'And welcome to the Hotel Matisse where we hope you will enjoy your stay...' And then the practised English phrase tailed off into hesitant foreign territory. 'I hope you will not be interrupted in your holiday by our many guests here. We have a wedding anniversary party this weekend and all the rooms – yours exceptionally – are taken up by the friends and relatives of the couple. Our booking person thought you were with the party when he got your reservation. I am sorry, it was a mistake, you should not have been accepted. The restaurant will not be open for you tomorrow night when the anniversary dance is held. If you would like I can offer you a room in our other hotel in Argeles. It may be quieter for you.'

Sensitive to the implication that he was of an age when he needed his sleep, Reynard bristled. 'No, that won't be necessary, thank-you. I will eat out tomorrow and try not to disturb your guests when I return,' he said with sarcasm that was lost on the receptionist.

By the time he had changed and wandered the quayside his mood had brightened, helped by the warmth of the late afternoon sun and an infusion of stark colours at every twist and turn, from the azure blue of the tide to the vulgar red of the geraniums in terracotta pots outside sunflower doors. That night he slept soundly despite the warmth, sent into a deep slumber with the help of a half bottle of red wine.

Reynard skipped breakfast – nerves had taken away his appetite and besides he intended taking his time preparing for what would be both his busking debut and his swansong. He shadow-practised La Mer, deftly fingering the ivory keys, humming along but holding back from squeezing the leather bellows. There was no need for him to hear the music. He had learnt it note for note, rehearsed it endlessly, could play it blindfolded in the middle of a traffic jam. This was to be his moment, and true to form he was mourning its passing already. The joy had been in the anticipation, the journey.

His train was about to pull into the station and the ride would be all over. He walked for an hour before carefully placing his case on the quayside and slowly, ceremoniously, taking out his squeezebox. He may as well have been taking out an Uzi machine gun for all the passing tourists noticed. Their aim was to tick off the vistas, the landmarks, to peruse the lunchtime menus, the men to glance surreptitiously at the lithe bodies on the beach below while their wives pretended not to notice. But he did it. Played La Mer twice. The first time, despite his earlier confidence with the song, he was nervous, faltered on a few notes and lost momentum, floundering like the pot-bellied swimmers in the bay who lacked technique to part the waves cleanly.

He couldn't let it end there, so he paused after the first rendition, pretended to adjust the keys, tied up his shoelaces and waited till the few holidaymakers who had stopped to listen gave up and continued their promenade. The next time he found his swing, in the music and in himself as he swayed from side to side. His joie de vivre was infectious and people were soon placing a coin on his case and chirping a 'tres bien'. As he began the final crescendo, the young receptionist from the hotel passed by and raised her eyebrows to him in exaggerated surprise, then broke into broad smile.

Reynard finished with a flourish but his own smile had faded before the last note. It was over, he thought to himself. The whole ridiculous episode. Now it was back to the real world and he wasn't sure he wanted to re-enter. As if to compound his thoughts he heard one of the spectators, a shaven-headed Englishman wearing a pair of pedal-pusher shorts and Manchester United shirt, muttering 'Only one song, I coulda done that.' There was no afterglow of achievement that he'd kidded himself he might feel. The pleasure had been in the planning, in secretly hoping his old colleagues would get wind of what he was up to and be knocked off their patronising little perches.

'What does it matter, anyway,' he whispered to himself as he finished of a second glass of a local red wine and settled his bill at the cafe-bar, inevitably once patronised by Picasso, according to a plaque on the wall.

He'd barely got through the door of the Hotel Matisse before the receptionist confronted him, slightly flushed and clearly embarrassed.

'Monsieur Reynard, thank goodness you are back, we are in much need of your help.'

Reynard, expecting some comeback from being spotted busking, drew in his breath in anticipation of being told he would after all be sent to the annexe. 'We need a musician to play for our guests, it is very important and we are desperate.'

Ignoring the impulse to say 'you must be' he listened as the receptionist explained that each year on this weekend Francoise and Henri Durand returned to celebrate their wedding anniversary. For the past six years, they and fifty of the same guests who had first toasted their wedding at the Hotel Matisse met again for a weekend of romance and reminiscence. And on the Saturday night the highlight was a wedding dinner exactly as it had been the first time round, followed by the bride and groom dancing to the Anniversary Song.

'It is their special moment,' said the receptionist with the hint of a tremble in her voice.

'And they insist on it being performed by two musicians who come here from a local village. They are a very romantic couple and they will be devastated that we cannot do it. The accordion player this afternoon slipped and broke his wrist.'

Reynard had turned ashen at the thought of what was coming next and started to splutter a refusal... 'No look, I can't… you see I can only… I'm not really music...'

But he was interrupted by an elegantly beautiful Francoise who had rushed from the restaurant to embrace him as her heaven-sent saviour from foreign fields.

'Monsieur, we are so happy you will play for us, thank you so much,' she gushed.

'But, I… hang on...' Reynard was destined not to finish a sentence. Henri Durand strode across the tiled floor to grab his flailing arm and shake it vigorously before hugging him even more enthusiastically and planting a kiss on both cheeks.

Reynard was swept into the restaurant on a wave of goodwill and a heady waft of Francoise's expensive perfume to meet the rest of the guests. To refuse now would not only be a crushing blow to immediate Anglo-French relations, it would condemn him to exile from his spiritual homeland. So in a toxic swill of wine-fuelled bonhomie and faltering Franglais, it was somehow agreed. Reynard would join the violinist for the grand moment, a duet of the Anniversary Song as Henri swept his beautiful bride around the floor.

As the last notes faded, the guests would join them for an encore. 'And that is it, Reynard. C'est fini. To do more would be, as you English say, egging over the cake,' said Francoise, in an accent that swept away any last thoughts in him of backing out.

It wasn't the wine that put Reynard into a cold sweat in the next hour. He was facing a public humiliation on a par with stepping out of the sea and strutting up the Collioure beach, sans trunks. Only this would be his lack of technique not his equipment that would be laid bare.

He struggled to recall the Anniversary Song, was it that dreadful record by Anita Harris in the Sixties, or was that the Anniversary Waltz? He sat in his room struggling to get any tune from his unco-operative squeezebox. He knew a few chords but any variations he tried as he pathetically attempted to sing 'may I always dance the anniversary waltz with you...' were unmistakably La Mer.

A rapping on the door broke into his desperation. He rose expecting to open it to a hostile guest who had rumbled his secret. To his greater shock it was a cheery-faced Frenchman looking like a character from a bad British sit-com, wearing a beret and Breton striped jumper, carrying what was unmistakably a violin case.

Gerard, 'the other musician' dressed to a stereotype but he was anything but. He had been a Paris businessman and spent much of his career in the City of London, before setting for a simpler life in the sun. He didn't need perfect English, which he was within touching distance of, to understand Reynard, who confessed all in one emotive outpouring. By the time he was finished, Gerard was near helpless with laughter, unable to offer the slightest comfort to Reynard who was now in a state of shock over his out-of-character soul-baring.

'I'm sorry, Reynard, it was the Anita Harris reference that did it. It is not the Anniversary Waltz but the Anniversary Song, different. Al Jolson, no? Listen...'

And he picked up his bow and played the mellow slow waltz of the Jolson classic, singing along, 'Oh, how we danced on the night we were wed...' Then with a wink that momentarily took away the twinkle in his eye, he upped the tempo to a 4/4 time and fiddled with the melody.

'But that's . . .' spluttered Reynard, still destined not to finish a sentence.

'Voila! From Anniversary to La Mer,' said Gerard triumphantly. 'Not exactement but very similar, you can do it too. It is perfect, it is fate but most of all, my friend, it is very funny to see an Englishman in a farce in France. An Anglais farce! Come, we will practise, but please do not sing like Mademoiselle Harris.'

At 11pm precisely the newly-formed duo stepped out to the edge of the dance-floor and the well-fed florid guests rose as one to applaud. They bowed modestly and the cheers rang out. Reynard with eyes fixed downward thought it excessive until nudged by Gerard who was pointing to the beaming Francoise and Henri who had left their table and were elegantly skipping to the floor. It was the cue to the couple's moments of bliss and what was to be Reynard's enduring happiness. The couple twirled and swooped, glided and gleamed as his playing merged seamlessly with Henri's soaring lead, sprinkling his runs like confetti on a warm summer breeze. The couple glowed, their guests pushed the rhythm with their clapping, Gerard winked again at Reynard and they flew. The squeezebox player didn't want to land but Gerard caught his eye with the signal to bring it in – knowing it would be the briefest of touchdowns before the excited guests would flood the floor for an encore performance. This time cheered on by a flushed Francoise who sat down next to the duo.

'It can't get any better than this,' Reynard thought. But as he played the final note of the encore, the guests remained on the floor, oddly silent after their raucous applause, looking pleased with themselves like children at a party with a shared secret. Francoise stood up and looked slyly at Reynard with a smile she couldn't quite hide.

'My friends, I am adding another tradition to our anniversary in honour of our English guest who stepped in to help us today, a foxtrot.

'Reynard and Gerard, please, La Mer.'

3.
Pinky and Perky

BLOODY Sunday. Sunday, bloody Sunday. It promised to be that all right.

A messy business when a copper gets stabbed in the back. For Detective Inspector Theo Monk the searing pain had given way to a deep grudge and no amount of self-administered medicine from a Scotch bottle was going to help. The staccato jazz piano of his musical hero and namesake, Thelonious Monk, which had so grated with his ex-wife and every girlfriend since, now did the same for him. Where he'd once heard harmony, he now felt discord: the barking of a black dog on his shoulder.

Today was Retribution Sunday. More blood was about to be spilled and this time it was Chief Superintendent Jeremy Watson who was donating, not him. Not a life-threatening amount, just enough to finish his career while keeping his pension intact.

'Serve the glory-hunting bastard right,' thought Monk, settling in to the park bench, relishing his carefully plotted revenge.

The timing had been crafted with the guile of a production down the road at Stratford-on-Avon. In Royal Leamington Spa, from a pocket park between the Royal Pump Rooms and the Royal Pavilion Shopping Centre, DI Monk was taking centre stage.

The Salvation Army Band was tuning up, as Monk knew it would be, bang on 8.50 am and would begin its march down the town's main thoroughfare, The Parade, at precisely 9am. His unwitting musical accomplices.

Traffic was starting to murmur on all three sides of the road-locked park, a tennis match was underway and an assortment of pampered dogs was being walked by equally well-groomed owners, each dutifully carrying a poop bag from the new dispenser bearing the slogan 'Don't mess with Royal Leam.'

Monk lit a Montecristo no.5 cigar, took a satisfying draw of the spiced Cuban tobacco and flicked away the match, attracting a disapproving stare from a passing poodle and owner, both blue-rinsed. Had he been in uniform, he could have expected to be pilloried in the letters column of the town's weekly newspaper. Not that the Courier would be in need of space-filling rants from readers this week. The red tops and heavies were publishing a story that would keep it in follow-ups for a month.

Monk's boss, Chief Supt. Watson, known behind his back as 'Ellie,' as in Elementary, dreary Watson, would be collecting his bundle of the Sundays in five minutes, on the dot. An obsessive when it came to routine, he had a typically self-serving reason for getting to the papers first. He scoured every page for mentions of himself.

And there were many these days, evidenced by the office back copies peppered with holes where once had been crime reports and sycophantic profiles. Now they were carefully indexed in his A3 leatherette Glory Folder.

The first inch of cigar ash fell on Monk's unfashionable trench coat as the band shuffled into line, feet stamped ready for the off. Monk pulled out his mobile. As if cued, the Sally Army struck up the hymn that by tradition started the spring processions and, with a collective jaunty step, marched towards him. Monk's mobile rang with the urgency of a 999 from the Palace.

He didn't need to look at the caller name to know it was Watson. Elementary. Who else would it be? He let it carry on ringing as the band, now in full cry, drew nearer. This was the moment he'd been relishing. Tenth ring, eleventh, twelfth. Lift Off. Answer the call.

'Good Morning, Chief Superintendent Watson…'

'Monk! You fuckin' little conniving bas…' Whatever else followed was lost in the soaring brass chorus of *All Things Bright and Beautiful* as the band passed Monk's outstretched arm. The sun broke cover from behind an oak bough, catching the rim of the lead trumpet at its moment of glory, sending a wink to the now beaming detective.

'Sorry Chief, I've lost you. Don't hear a word you're saying,' he shouted at the phone.

An hour later the now soothing piano of Thelonious Monk seeped from the top floor flat in a restored Victorian mansion, one of the few in town not converted to a nursing home. Soothing to DI Monk, that is, not his neighbours. The pianist's keyboard attack was accompanied by a violent syncopated rapping on his front door. Monk had no intention of opening it.

He wasn't scared of Watson, only afraid that he'd spoil his triumph by clocking the bastard for good measure and find himself on an assault charge. Besides he was engrossed in exchanging emails with Dayle Scooter, the local freelance reporter, who'd booked a five-day break in New York on the back of today's handiwork in the Sunday papers.

Monk was pleased for the lad. He'd played his part well. The pay-off would more than make up for Scooter losing what should have been the biggest payday of his career, scuppered when Watson tipped off his contacts in Fleet Street about a sensational trial at Warwick Crown Court.

In Scooter's daily grind on the Midland court circuit the staples were frauds, rapes, GBH and robberies. But for the most part the crimes, though serious enough in themselves, were not going to interest tabloid news editors who were more excited by a soap star being given a driving ban by Marylebone magistrates.

Scooter earned most of his modest income from local papers and radio stations unwilling to spare one their own reporters to sit in court all day. So they paid him £50 to do it when a juicy trial came up. That arrangement didn't mean Scooter was duty bound to tell them about a cracker like the Pinky and Perky drugs case. Not until he'd filed copy to his more affluent London paymasters, anyway. A dead cert national story came his way maybe once a year; one like this with tabloid and broadsheet appeal was even scarcer.

The earlier committal hearings had given nothing away about the story that was to unfold. Scooter had it to himself and he intended to have it sizzling down the wires to London news editors as soon as the prosecution QC sat down from outlining the case to the jury.

At least, that had been the intention. But he'd arrived at court to be met by a phalanx of reporters jostling in the queue for the Press Bench while their snappers loitered in the surrounding streets taking snatch shots of anyone who looked like a defendant, including three elderly clergymen whose hasty but innocent scuttle towards the court made them guilty in the eyes of the cameramen.

Their plea that they were simply late for morning service at the adjoining parish church of St Margaret made no difference.

Watson had primed the Press well. But he'd made two powerful enemies in Scooter and Monk in doing so. Monk had long known Watson as a greasy-pole climber of Olympic class. But he wasn't going to let him get away with using his back for a lift up onto the podium.

By looking after his friends in the Press, Watson had, of course, been looking out for number one even better, lining himself to claim every last morsel of credit for bringing the Pinky and Perky gang to book. His faults were many but failure to leap on a bandwagon pulled by a gift horse was not one of them. Especially when it could give his already-high public profile a shove along the road to Chief Constable. The P&P investigation, Monk's case, as the whole force knew, had grabbed the attention of the world's media, particularly those specialising in boosting circulation in the Nether Regions.

Infiltrating an international drugs ring can be a fatal attraction for a cop. Maverick detectives poking their noses in have ended up supporting the footings of a new office block or bobbing up in the Channel wearing their own handcuffs.

DI Monk's trail to the Pinky and Perky gang began with his choking in the beer garden of The Ferret in Warwick. He was only three gulps into his pint of Ramparts Revenge when he gagged, spraying Benny the Savage in the process.

'You're making this one up, Benny. I can see the bloody smirk even under that ridiculous black paint,' Monk spluttered.

In fact, Benny was expressionless, although it was hard to tell beneath the glutinous make-up smeared across his entire face, framed by a pulled-down battered top hat. Only the tinkling rustle of his shredded headmaster's gown adorned with turkey feathers and cow bells betrayed his indignation.

'Steady on, Theo, have a listen first before you take a pot at the outfit. We Morris Men from the Borders are proud of our blackface tradition. Goes back centuries, you know.

Monk knew only too well. It was Benny's trap to lure

Pinky and Perky

him into his favourite game, already played out with a gullible tourist in town for the folk festival.

The visitor always made the opening move. Usually a tentative remark about the appropriateness of blackface in this day and age; sometimes a hostile attack accusing Benny of blatant racism.

Benny first trots out the party line about a tradition that was started by poor serfs disguising themselves while moonlighting as minstrels, fearful of being recognised by their day-job masters. It was plausible enough to keep his accuser hooked while he casually threw out another piece of bait along the lines of 'shifting perspectives' and 'white man's guilt.'

As his prey flapped about in indignation, Benny reeled him in, theatrically taking off his gloves and rubbing his brow with a wet wipe to reveal his true colour. A mellow light brown.

'I'm about a Spice Tea on the Dulux colour swatch, part of the Orange Family of shades, apparently,' he tells his incredulous accuser.

'You look midway between an Ivory Blush and Warm Stone. Ten years ago I would have been mid brown and you pink. They are just labels, not a problem unless you want them to be.'

Satisfied that he had check-mate, Benny, who as far as Monk knew or cared grew up on the border of Solihull and Brum like his father before him, then leaned back with a friendly smile for his opponent, signalling end of conversation. Monk had seen the act too many times to be impressed.

'Let's just get this clear, Benny. Just in case I'm hallucinating. You're asking me to believe that the folk festival will be awash with a new drug known as a Pinky and Perky, so called because of the revitalising effect it has on middle-aged men's rhythm-sticks? Even by your standards, that is a loada bloody bollocks.'

Benny raises a blackened eyebrow at the detective's unintentional but roughly accurate image of what had befallen folkies who had overdosed on P&Ps.

'To be precise, Theo, the name comes from its two main elements: Korean red ginseng, an expensive aphrodisiac, which when cut with third cocaine comes out with a pinkish tint. And super-strength Viagra, known as Pandgra, developed for a zoo in china to make 20-stone giant pandas more, er, perky.

'At £50 a tablet, there's a fortune to be made at festivals. But it's high risk, there have been deaths.'

Monk slammed down his glass, emptying it of the few dregs that hadn't been lost in the earlier spraying.

'Benny, if you're going to crack that old gag about them pole-vaulting out the bedroom window in a state of over excitement you're bloody nicked for wasting police time.'

'Cardiac arrests,' Benny replies. 'Think about it. Why target folk festivals? Because by and large, mainly large, there are thousands of middle-aged men there who enjoy the good things in life. Singing, sticking an index finger in the ear, growing beards, drinking beer, singing about fair maidens, drinking beer. And when they get home to the missus the effect of the ale on their already flagging libidos leaves them pushing a rope uphill, so to speak. A Pinky and Perky guarantees they can provide 24-hour non-stop service, using revitalised equipment. A bit like the RAC man with a reconditioned tow-truck, if you like. But it puts too much strain on the ticker. The Hampton Gusset Morris Dancers lost three of their best last month to heart attacks.'

He pauses, teeing up his punch line: 'Their members just couldn't take it.'

Monk explodes in fury. 'I bloody knew it! It's a wind up, you black-faced bastard.'

The young couple on the next table leap to their feet in indignation, the man admonishing Monk as they leave. 'You ought to ashamed; my grandfather fought a world war to rid us of racists like you.'

'Sorry, Theo,' says Benny. 'Couldn't resist throwing that one in. But it's all true. Check the figures with coroners and I'll bet you'll find a steep rise in fatal heart attacks in areas with festivals like these.

'Only they'll be recorded as natural causes. Sad thing is most of the victims were probably due a heart attack, anyway. Pinky and Perky just speeded things up a bit. Terrible embarrassment for the families. No wonder they try to keep a lid on it. Funeral directors had the same problem with the coffins, evidently.'

He pre-empts another Monk attack by swiftly adding, 'Okay, okay, no more jokes. Everything else is absolutely kosher. And if you and your flatfeet crew want to see for yourselves put on your dancing shoes.'

Monk still thought it was a Benny wind-up when he got back to the office. But nevertheless he told one of the eager PCs to get stats together from coroners in six counties that had staged festivals. He didn't specify folk, these days any music festival was a magnet for grandparents. Glasto had introduced crowd-surfing classes for grey-hairs at the Old Gits Stage, and Dropdedery barred under 40s unless escorting a relative over 65.

When the numbers had been crunched and compared to fatal heart attacks the previous year, Monk started to believe. There had been a rise of 454 deaths. Something was up. And if it wasn't Pinky and Perky causing it, then the consumption of crisps and ale must have increased 100-fold. Death by natural greed? Or manslaughter by illegal drugs of 450-plus folkies? Monk aimed to find out.

That Saturday morning at Warwick Folk Festival, only fans of Benny the Savage and his Blackface Stickers, of which there were nine, counting wives, would have noted an extra Sticker in the team. Neither they nor anyone in the crowd lining Market Square for the opening parade would have recognised DI Theo Monk beneath the thick layer of black slap. They may have thought, however, that his bulging paunch, a settee cushion taped beneath his gown and fur waistcoat, didn't seem in proportion to his otherwise lean frame.

'Looking good, Brother Sticker,' Benny goaded, holding his stick 'in the horizontal' across his loins. Monk copied the ritual greeting, and, as instructed, took a step back and swung it to smash against Benny's shin-pad as

Pinky and Perky

his mentor's stick hit his, rather more forcefully.

The ensuing events were to form vital evidence at the trial, having first survived an accusation of entrapment by the defence. Monk was ready for that. He made a virtue of the fact he'd dressed as a fearsome Sticker, causing at least three children to cry during the parade, as proof that he'd looked as approachable as a rabid pit-bull.

The prosecution played video and sound recordings to the jury, proving Monk was doing nothing more provocative than puffing on a Montecristo no. 5 outside the Castle Antique Emporium during a lull in dancing when a pink-faced heavily sweating Morris Man sidled up to him.

'Not much you can see down south with that beer-gut blocking your view,' he said, taking off his flowered straw boater and patting his own sizable paunch in empathy. Out of sight out of mind, eh? Bloody shame though, when you get to the stage when you've got the rumpy but no pumpy.'

Monk was too wily to ask him what he would suggest. He took a meaningful draw of cigar smoke and, making sure he was facing away from WPC Love, who was posing as a tourist shooting a video across the street, nodded resignedly.

The dealer, 'call me Porker,' wasn't as dumb as he looked thereafter. He didn't have the drugs on him. The M.O., he explained, was that Monk would go with him into the Cavalier Cafe, buy his new pal a coffee and hand him the change.

'£50, so you might want to go to the cash point first,' Porker said in a high squeaky voice with a trace of a Cotswolds burr.

He would leave after a few sips of coffee, instructing Monk to sit tight. Within seconds a sour-faced waitress would come over and wipe the table, leaving a small brown sugar pack on his saucer.

'Don't drop that in your coffee, my friend,' was Porker's departing advice, 'or you won't be able to get your lower half out from under the table.'

WPC Love was kept busy that afternoon, filming fifteen other clients buying Porker a coffee.

'No wonder he only took a few sips each time,' she told a de-blacked Monk back at the nick.

The rest of the surveillance team, detective constables Jim 'Jammy' Lodger and Dazzer O'Brien, had an easier task in tailing Porker. Until they reached the sixth boozer when Porker showed his criminal nous, and despite the handicap of a beer-barrel belly slipped out the back door of the Codpiece and Eel.

'Count yourself bloody lucky that Benny was taking a leak in the yard when the bugger got in the motor,' Monk berated them. If he hadn't phoned me with the reg number you'd be posting Neighbourhood Watch leaflets through letterboxes tomorrow.'

The two detectives took their bollockings in silence, trying not to look into Monk's panda eyes, the result of black make-up residue he'd missed. They knew that Monk hadn't relied on the car to trace Porker. He'd pocketed the spoon the dealer had used to stir his coffee and had it run through fingerprinting.

'Reggie Montgomery, builder by trade, villain by inclination,' Monk announced.

'Did very well indeed for himself in Gloucestershire building houses and renovating Cotswold cottages. Quite legit. Apart from forgetting to tell the Inland Revenue how well he was doing, by the odd million. He spent six months in Ford Open for tax dodging.

'Not major league stuff and six months holiday wouldn't have been so bad given that his assets had long been transferred to his wife and couldn't be clawed back.

'But she took a shine to Reggie's apprentice brickie while hubby was taking creative writing classes at Ford and they are presently enjoying each others' company and his money in Spain.'

The squad knew that nailing Porker would be the easy bit. Following the chain of command was going to a lot tougher and mean watching the dealer's backside 24/7. The prospect was daunting but more appealing than the other arse that butted in to the investigation the next day: Chief Super Watkins. He ordered an update report on his desk by 4pm every day and a phone call from Monk at 8pm with any breaking leads. His aim, all too clear to Monk, was to hijack the investigation without lifting a finger. Monk knew Watson would have that report retyped under his own name and on the Chief Constable's desk by 5pm and be calling him at 9am with the overnight progress, throwing in a few yawns to give the impression that he'd been up until the small hours with the surveillance crew. He was right. After two days the Chief was so impressed he appointed Watson co-ordinator of Operation Pinky and Perky with a brief to liaise with Interpol and the International Drug Enforcement Agency.

Watson had secured the stage. Or so he thought.

In the days after the festival it became clear to Monk that he wasn't dealing with Colombian drug overlords infiltrating his patch or heavyweight gangsters from Manchester or London. This was a far rarer type of a Mr Big. The gifted amateur. A maverick that probably had no form at all. Clever too. He was pulling the strings of Pinky and Perky by invisible threads. Surveillance of Porker and the dozen other dealers revealed them as a disparate rag-bag of town hall pen-pushers, students, self-employed builders and lorry drivers with no common thread, other than spending their weekends selling narcotics. Porker was the best qualified in as much as he had a bit of form but was at most team leader, sales. How they got their Pinky & Perkys, and where the money ended up was still a mystery to Monk three days into the investigation. He wasn't going to tell Watson that. If he chose to interpret his sly references to an 'eastern connection' as a hint that a sophisticated gang, bankrolled by laundered roubles, was operating and embellish it for the Chief's ears, that was up to him.

Benny had been no further east than Great Yarmouth for a freezing holiday fortnight as a child. The last resort he'd go to nowadays. He was Monk's last resort, though. Professional pride had stopped him ringing before.

Pinky and Perky

Benny had handed him a sensational case on a plate and all he'd managed so far was to nibble around the edges. Porker was merely a starter; he hadn't got close to the meat of the matter.

Benny answered the call on the third ring, anticipating the question and ready with an answer. But not yet.

'How's it going, Monk? Charged 'em yet? Am I speaking to newly-promoted Superintendent Theo Monk?'

'No you're effing not you smug sod,' Monk replies. 'As you bloody well know. We've hit a wall. This lot may be weekend crooks but whoever's pulling the strings is a clever bastard. I'd got to the point where you were prime suspect; then I knew I was floundering. You know things, Benny, I need a bit more.'

The pause on the other end of the line was broken by a theatrical sigh. 'Truth is Monk, I told you all I know. But don't underestimate the Morris Men. They may look to you like a bunch of saddos prancing about waving hankies but they are drilled with military precision.

'My guess is there are whole teams working the operation. Take a closer look at their dancing and in particular watch out for the Fool, the Beast and the Bagman. But don't fall for the Fool's distracting antics.'

Monk knew about the Fool's role from his stand in with the Stickers. He wouldn't have thought it possible to look more ridiculous than a troop of overweight men with blackened faces dressed as if they had been through a combine harvester. But the Fool managed it. He added a pink baby doll nightie to his ensemble and shook an oversized baby rattle. He acted like an opportunistic gatecrasher, upstaging his fellow Stickers by wisecracking to the bemused audience and weaving a manic jig through the orderly Morris dancers. A useful foil, thought Monk, if something is going on elsewhere.

Monk had already scrutinised all the Bagmen, the most obvious players to be the temporary holding bank. They were the Morris Men's treasurers, keeping hold of the teams' watches, wallets and phones when the dances began. But neither Porker nor the other dealers went near them during the dance.

As for the Beast, as far as Monk could figure out it was a dancer dressed up as a mythical animal or legendary hero that tagged along to entertain the kids by frightening the life out of them. About par for the course. Not all teams had them, perhaps only one or two at the festival that he'd seen. A Green Man, champion of the forest, sort of Robin Hood for veggies but looking like Worzel Gummidge wearing an Incredible Hulk costume. And, from what he could recall, the other was a panto cow, supposed to be a Dun Cow, the mythical giant Ox that roamed the fields of merrie olde Warwickshire trampling homesteads and goring knights.

Monk lit a Montecristo, took a draw, put on his thinking cap, then lifted the internal phone.

'Love, get all the footage you've got and have it ready in the screening room in 30 minutes. Bring along Dodger and Dazzer and as many flasks of coffee you can get from the canteen. It's going to be a long night.'

The trio looked beaten before they'd begun. More than

Pinky and Perky

eighteen hours of video to scour frame by frame, looking for a big cow and a green giant. Six hours in and two flasks of coffee later they got a brief sighting of the green man, trying to calm a bawling child. Another two hours and eyes that had fought to stay open were reduced to thin slits, partly the result of staring at a screen for so long but more the effect of smoke from ten exhaled Cuban cigars from Monk's pursed lips. Dodger's breathing was beginning to sound like a soft snore.

From out of the fug, Monk's sharp command brought them round: 'Freeze the cow!'

'Now back a few frames,' he ordered as the detectives stared at a figure that could have been taken for ZZ Top's roadie, had he not been wearing a huge pair of buffalo horns on his head and a lurid wobbly cow's udder strapped to his belly.

'There, got 'em both,' shouted Monk. The unmistakable figure of Porker appeared from the crowd, stumbled, then bumped into the cow, appearing to steady himself by grabbing the udder. At that moment the Fool diverted the crowd's attention and WPC Love's camera by bunny hopping between the dancers while forcing rude noises out of a kazoo.

In his moment of triumph, Monk barked an order to Dodger and Dazzer which would pass down in police folklore: 'Get on the tail of that fucking cow.'

They didn't have to. Benny gave them a bigger steer. 'The Dun Cow is the Beast of the Lighthorne Leggers Morris Men,' he said coolly to Monk's excited question. 'Who would have thought it?' It was rhetorical, an intonation that hadn't gone unnoticed by Monk. 'New team, relatively, formed a few years ago by a guy called Duncan Silverside, works at the vegetable research centre.

'Clever bugger, always thought he was taking the piss out of the whole thing. I think I was the only one who sussed his Dun Cow.'

Monk was furious. 'So you knew about the drugs all along? That's a criminal offence, Benny, you're in trouble.'

'Steady, Monk. I meant the name. Dun Cow...Dun-can Silverside, as in beef. Geddit?'

Silverside lived alone in what had been a tied cottage for sewage plant managers at Scabbard's Heath. The water authority had sold it off after making the maintenance engineer redundant, and homeless, when the plant became automated, although not odour free. A feature which kept the selling price down and visitors few and far between. Its relative isolation posed a problem for DCs Lodger and O'Brien who spent five days as road-workers replacing kerbstones to get close enough to monitor comings and goings. They were right in thinking they'd got the shitty end of the stick. Monk had got wind of them shooting their mouths off about his 'tail the cow' faux pas and he suspected both of them were in the pocket of Watson. Their detail wasn't quite a fool's errand however. But it was a punishment nevertheless.

Monk and WPC Love had the pointy end of the stick and were about to skewer Mr Pinky and Perky with it. Monk had been impressed by Love's attention to detail during the investigation, and flattered when she had asked him if his parents were jazz fans, thinking she must have taken the trouble to do a bit of research on him. It turned out she hadn't, she was a bit of a bebop fan and anyone with a passing acquaintance with jazz would have known of Thelonious Monk.

WPC Love became Amanda after that first off-duty drink together. Monk felt trusting enough to reveal that 'Theo' was a nickname bestowed on him at university when his newly-acquired mates thumbed through his record collection. His real name was Henry, so he wasn't complaining.

By the time Silverside sat in front of them, under caution, Monk knew they had him like a fish in a barrel. His boss, the chief executive of the Vegetable Research Station, had been extremely candid when Monk and Love had arrived for preliminary enquiries. He made it clear he disliked Silverside, his head of research for disease resistant crops in Southeast Asia.

'Duncan is one of our most experienced and respected scientists,' he told them in a tone that said otherwise.

'But he's not an easy man to get along with. The staff turnover in his department is considerable. The running joke in HR is we need to develop a strain of Duncan-resistant young scientists or we'll be wiped out.

'He's just not a team player, even keeps some labs locked, out of bounds to everyone bar himself. Wouldn't get away with it but for the fact he's the best in his field.

Monk let him release a bit more steam before asking what precisely Silverside was working on. The answer didn't require the powers of Sherlock Holmes to deduce they had found their Mr Big.

'His major project is helping the Chinese government to preserve the country's biggest tourist draw, the Giant Panda. One of Nature's contradictions, the Panda. It's got the gut of a carnivore but eats nothing but bamboo, up to 14 hours a day.

'No wonder it's got the libido of a eunuch. The Chinese have come up with a solution that seems to be working with zoo pandas, basically a combination of sildenafil - Viagra to you - and more controversially the leaf of the coca, or cocaine.

'The problem is getting it to the client in the wild. Duncan is working on a spray that will coat the bamboo without affecting its nutritional value, and most importantly won't turn every insect that lands on it into a six-legged sex maniac.'

There was more than enough to initiate a search warrant of all the labs and Silverstone's home. Monk offered to bet the first round of drinks with Amanda Love that they would find red ginseng growing in one of the locked labs and batches of Pandgra sent from China, probably in officially-sanctioned sealed metal containers, at his home. She refused, but countered with an offer to listen to his record collection if he was right.

She didn't get drinks or the music that night. Chief Supt Watson had been tipped off about the search by the two DCs he'd been cultivating, and insisted that he would lead the raid on Silverside's cottage.

'You've got enough on him already to convict a bloody Pope of drug dealing. Arrest your man and bring him in,' he'd bellowed down the phone at Monk.

It wasn't the way Monk wanted to play it. But Ellie had spoken, which was more than Silverside did when they sat him down in the interview room back at the station.

He hadn't shown a flicker of surprise when confronted by Monk and Love, sarcastically offering his wrists for cuffing, and smiling at open-mouthed colleagues watching him being led away.

'I am not answering any questions other than to confirm who I am until my lawyer is present,' he said, with the aloofness of an Oxford Don addressing primary school pupils. He pretended to straighten his Windsor-knotted silk tie, glanced at an expensive but not showy wristwatch, stared Monk in the eye, and said nothing more.

'For a bloke who sticks on a ZZ Top beard,' Monk began, 'wears a pair of cow horns on his head and straps a floppy udder to his chest, I'd expected more of a performance.'

Silverside tensed, his eyelids broke cover and blinked, but he remained mute. Monk decided to get in a few more blows, not because it would help the investigation. He'd just taken an instant dislike to the man.

'Did you develop Pinky and Perky for your own use initially, Mr Silverside? Or had you retired from active service, as it were, when your wife walked out on you after 30 years of marriage?'

Even WPC Love winced at that one. A bit rich coming from someone whose wife had done the same, she thought. Silverside bit his tongue.

'Sorry, bit below the belt,' Monk said unconvincingly.

'Still, not so bad when you can ease the misery by giving pleasure to thousands of other women, by proxy. The earth certainly moved for them all right. And for their husbands, although in their case it was soil for a six-foot grave.'

Monk had his man down. Silverside's face betrayed him; his eyes were watery and Monk thought he heard a sniffle. The detective was satisfied. He didn't need to break him. The evidence was overwhelming, there was no wriggle room for Silverside to exploit. He'd be charged with the importation of illegal substances to start with. Then it would be up to the Crown Prosecution Service to decide if there was a strong enough case to hold him to account for the heart attack deaths.

Murder charges had already been ruled out, although Monk had argued that as a biological scientist, Silverside must have known the fatal potential of the drug he was peddling. Monk pinned his hopes on manslaughter for at least four of the deaths. But the CPS wasn't convinced on that either. In a recent case involving the death of an addict, the judge threw out the case on the grounds that if the victim knowingly took an illegal drug then he bore the responsibility for the consequences, not the supplier.

Monk resigned himself to the probability the gang would stand trial on drugs offences only. But that could

Pinky and Perky

still mean Silverside getting up to 14 years for importing, Porker maybe seven years and his runners three or four.

Silverside never uttered a word during the formal interviews that followed his arrest, in the outdated belief that a 'no comment' couldn't be held against him. His arrogance brokered no advice from his lawyer to the contrary.

It didn't impress the jury. Silverside had pleaded not guilty to the illegal importation of controlled drugs and would offer no evidence in defence, his embarrassed barrister informed the court. Porker and the crew had pleaded guilty to their roles at a separate trial and would be sentenced at a later date. In order that their pleas wouldn't influence the jury for Silverside, their pleas could not be reported or referred to.

That scrupulous balancing of the scales of justice was easily tipped off kilter by the defendant's refusal to give evidence. The verdict was a foregone conclusion and it was a puzzle to seasoned lawyers that such a blatant waste of the court's time hadn't by now earned the judge's condemnation. On the contrary, His Honour Sebastian Grudge-Fortune seemed to want to spin it out, frequently stopping the prosecutor for what seemed to the jury rather unnecessary details about the minutiae of Pinky and Perky's qualities.

After each clarification, the judge emitted a sigh of surprise followed by an arched eyebrow and a muttered 'really?' as he scribbled furtive notes on his yellow pad. None of the jurors had difficulty understanding the forensic expert's evidence and were puzzled by the judge's ever-reddening face and heavy breathing as each point was laboured.

His behaviour soon attracted the attention of the sketch writers who comfortably found five hundred words each day to make a colourful sidebar to their newspapers' main reports.

As the trial entered its second week it became almost impossible to discern which was which. Bickering broke out among the hacks over who should report the performance of the prosecution's expert witness, Professor Mike Charning, whose published works on the origins of English folklore and customs included essays on the symbolism of the Morris Dance. Charning was only just hitting his stride, warming up the jury, as he thought, with a detailed description of the Morris Men's costume and lamenting the use of plastic flowers in the hat, when the judge interjected.

'And what, please enlighten us, is the purpose of wearing a silly hat and prancing about like Bavarian nancy-boys waving a white hanky?'

The academic, taking it as a brutal attack on English tradition and by implication his own raison d'être, paused stone-faced, staring in turn at the prosecution barrister in his silks and prim wig and then at the judge, regaled in scarlet robes and precisely coiffured artificial grey locks.

'Your Honour, many of us believe that a costume lends an air of authority and reassuring credibility to proceedings, whether in the field of law or in England's green meadows around a Maypole. But it is true that some think that slipping on a bright gown and a powdered hairpiece is a manifestation of the Englishman's fetish for women's clothing, rooted in an upbringing by nannies.'

The Press Bench let out a collective guffaw, jurors sniggered and the public gallery burst out in undisguised laughter punctuated with hoots of 'hear, hear!

'Silence in court, silence I say.' The judge's face was by now as red as his robe. 'I will not have this court turned into a pantomime.' His admonishment immediately undermined by a slipping wig covering his eyes.

The headline writers thought all their birthdays had come at once and not content with puns involving pandas, erections, Pinky and Perky and Mr Big, decided to award a bottle of Champagne for the week's most contrived effort. The Sun edged it with a picture of a cardiac arrest casualty and a cut-out of Pinky and Perky under the banner: 'Zing went the strings of his heart'. The strapline: 'Wife wanted Giant Panda-ing but ended up with a Stiff in bed,' was duly condemned by the Press Complaints Commission as insensitive, earning the writer a second bonus bottle of bubbly from colleagues. Meanwhile the Guardian did its customary seizure of the high moral ground by reporting on the tabloids' reports in a censorious tone, thus ensuring that its readers didn't miss out on the pun-fest but could still tut-tut about the gutter press.

As the trial dragged on, however, the interest began to sag. Without Silverside taking the stand, the panto was denied its villain. A case that started with a bang desperately needed a second front to maintain the bombardment of the nation's incredulity. DI Monk stepped into the breach from the witness box, giving an authoritative account of the China connection and how the Perkys were shipped in sealed containers bearing warnings about toxic medical material, then returned the same way with the contents swapped for bundles of £50 notes.

'The recipient, an official with the Giant Panda Reserve in central China, is currently being sought by the authorities on suspicion of embezzlement and drug smuggling.'

Monk paused. Then, gaze fixed on the Press Bench, added, 'And money laundering.'

Even the Times, which had steadfastly refused to join in the punning found it impossible to resist headlining the next day's report: 'Chinese Laundry Washed Pinky and Perky Drugs Cash,' while the Mail set the pace with 'Oh, Mr Wu, what a to-do, he's run off with the Chinese Laundry dues.'

Monk's quotes ensured front page coverage once more, picking up heroic embellishments to his rank along the way from a grateful Press. 'Super sleuth who headed the Pinky and Perky investigation,' was one in particular that had been noted by Chief Supt Jeremy Watson, whose scissors had lain idle in his drawer throughout the trial. He swore to himself that he would gain the initiative once the guilty verdict was in. Meanwhile, the Chief Constable and the chairman of the police authority were also deeply troubled at the way the story was being handled. Monk had done a first rate job, they agreed, but Watson had made the force look foolish with his suggestions that Pinky and Perky was the brainchild of an international drug mafia. The Chief had conveniently forgotten who had instructed Watson to alert Interpol.

Adding to the embarrassment, leading articles were appearing sympathising with sufferers of middle-age impotence, hypocritically questioning the brutal way the issue was being held up to ridicule. Pressure groups like RISE – Research into Sexual Expectation – and DAD – Dead Against Droop - were supplying a constant stream of couples willing to talk about their bedroom anguish, while showing no hesitation in sticking it up the Press for their treatment of the issue. The families of several Pinky and Perky victims shed anonymity and weighed in to rail against the police for exposing their loved ones to ridicule. Condemnation was heaped on the force after a police officer on duty outside Warwick Crown Court was confronted by an angry protester shouting 'My husband will be turning in his grave at this fiasco' and retorted 'I'd be surprised if he could manage that, love.'

Damage limitation was now paramount. The Chief Constable issued a stern memo to all serving officers, reminding them that he expected the highest standards when dealing with sensitive issues raised by the case.

'There must be no joining in with the schoolboy humour that had distracted from a serious crime, which has, in the final reckoning, contributed to loss of lives,' he wrote. All press enquiries would henceforth be referred directly to him and no exceptions.

Chief Supt Jeremy Watson read the order with only slight apprehension. He intended to grab what glory was left, come what may. He started with a phone call to Scooter during the court lunch-break.

'Dayle, no hard feelings, I hope, about the national boys stealing your thunder. Bound to happen really, can't keep this one under wraps.'

Scooter was seething. 'Just for the opening day I could've and it would've made the difference between £50 and £5,000. I wasn't interested in the thunder, only a windfall, unlike some people…'

'Well, water under the bridge now, Dayle. I come offering you a chance to claw back a bit of what's passed you by. An exclusive one-to-one interview with me on the tracking down of the P&P gang, for publication the day after the formality of the guilty verdict.

'What's the catch?'

'Just this. The interview took place yesterday, if you are asked, and you filed it to the nationals the same day. Got it?'

Scooter got it all right. He'd seen a leaked copy of the Chief Constable's memo only an hour ago. Monk had sent it.

That evening Scooter and Monk, despite the aggressive piano of Thelonious Monk constantly intruding into the conversation, concocted a plan.

'Bloody hell, what a racket, who the hell is giving the old Joanna grief,' Scooter had remarked when he stepped into Monk's flat.

'One of the greatest jazz musicians of the 20th century,

Thelonious Monk. I take it you're not familiar with his work?'

'No but I've heard of William Henry Monk who wrote *All Things Bright and Beautiful*,' Scooter laughed. 'I only know that because I had to choose the music for Dad's funeral and the one thing he loved was hearing the Sally Army play that song at the start of their march from the park. I had to take him there, 9am every Sunday in spring, regular as clockwork.'

Monk didn't answer, just stared vacantly at his fellow conspirator while the cogs started to whirl. Scooter was about to ask him if he would like a glass of water, when Monk poured two generous tumblers of malt.

'Scooter you're brilliant and if you weren't so bloody ugly I'd kiss you.'

Had Monk been a fly on the wall the next morning at Scooter's interview with Watson, he would have been obliged to hand him the whole bottle and French kiss him for his performance. As expected, Watson gave chapter and verse about the investigation, substituting his own name for Monk's. He claimed it was one of his snouts in the swill of Warwick's underworld who first tipped him off. No names, no pack drill but he knows who he is. Diligent detective work had untied the tangled web (a token sop to the team he nominally led), but the China connection required a great deal of diplomacy, and he was honoured that the Chief Constable had asked him personally to oversee that role.

He leaned forward to Scooter, speaking slowly and

deliberately to emphasise the nugget he was delivering: 'I am delighted to announce that the zoo and the Chinese government are so grateful to the British police for breaking this drugs ring, which threatened to heap disgrace on their nation, they will name the next pandas born at the zoo Sherlock and Watson.

'Sheer coincidence about my name, of course,' Watson said unconvincingly. 'It's an honour for the whole Warwickshire force, not just me.'

An hour into the interview and three pints apiece of Ramparts' Revenge downed, Scooter took control with a textbook performance of the dark arts of reportage.

'Chief Super,' he began matily. 'This is a brilliant story and just the sort of backgrounder the nats will be begging for come Friday. The trial is bound to end then. The jury has to be out for a minimum 90 minutes, so they'll have 88 minutes to twiddle their thumbs before coming back in with a guilty verdict by midday. That gives us a problem.'

'I don't recognise problems Scooter, just challenges,' responded Watson, in slightly slurred management speak.

'Well it's this, the verdicts and sentence will be all over TV and radio; Saturday's papers will concentrate on the result. Your interview is a great follow-up, a natural for the Sundays, the real story behind the Pinky and Perky gang, by the top cop who tracked them down.

'But, and it's a big but, readers will expect to read your reaction to the verdict and sentence. But that would let the cat out the bag, that you'd given an interview after the ban on speaking to the Press was imposed.'

'I see what you mean Scooter. But I not a greenhorn when it comes to the workings of the Press, lad. You can have a standard police-speak reaction and send it over as an add to the main story. Tell the editors to put it as a sidebar and I'll make it sound like a statement from the force.

'Take this down: "It is for the court to decide the punishment. As servants of the Crown, it is our job to bring them before a jury with the fullest possible facts. Our sympathy is extended to the families of the victims of this drugs racket. But let this be a warning to drugs barons whether they are from China, Columbia or Scabbard's Heath. You will be caught and jailed if you ply your deadly trade in Warwickshire".'

Scooter ordered another two pints and in a calculated aside baited his trap: 'You'll be pretty pissed off if Silverside gets less than nine years, though.'

Three pints before, the detective in Watson, what there was of it, might have smelt a rat; noticed how that young couple on the nearby table had stopped cooing into each other's ears. He might also have seen the woman carefully point her handbag in his direction but he wouldn't have seen the omni-directional microphone hidden in the buckle. The undercover reporters' subterfuge wasn't necessary. The drink was talking now. Very loudly.

'Pissed off? I'd be flaming livid. Silverside should have had the book thrown at him. He's got away with murder, or at least manslaughter. The bloody court should increase the maximum for what he's done to twenty years, in my view.

'They've gone soft on drug dealers, that's all the Pinky and Perky mob are. Stick 'em away for a long stretch, they won't have much use for Viagra in pokey!'

The covert reporters along with a small gathering of regulars standing at the bar burst into laughter and gave a spontaneous round of applause. Watson, realising his double entendres, joined in himself, carried away by the reaction like a karaoke singer who thinks he's a star.

'Look what happens when you handle them with kid gloves!' he appealed to his audience, throwing in a lewd wink.

'Porker had six months in a bloody holiday camp called an open prison taking friggin pottery classes and writing poems. Fat lot of good that did him.

'He and the rest of the motley crew should be given a hard time. They deserve a good stiff sentence not a pat on the back from a limp-wristed judge!'

Scooter closed his notebook and gave a sympathetic shrug, a shorthand gesture intended to signal that the outburst wasn't going in his report.

'Not in mine but someone else's,' he thought, ostentatiously checking his watch, then sticking out his hand in apparent recognition of Watson's bravado.

'Courts reconvening in 10 minutes, we're on the summing up, won't be long now," Scooter said departing.

Watson nodded but he wasn't going yet, not while there was still a near-full pint undrunk. As he dipped a tired head to his tankard the two undercover reporters were at the door, quietly pointing him out to their snapper before themselves leaving.

Scooter had done their spade work. He'd sent their news editor a copy of the Chief Constable's warning and later he would be filing his interview, minus the outburst. That would be written by the two staffers for a front page splash. His arse was covered. The other papers would be furious at being scooped but it wasn't his fault if rival reporters got lucky hanging around in a pub, was it?

For once Scooter didn't mind that his byline wouldn't be used. He might be out in the sticks but he was as sharp as a Cockney's tiepin and knew how they'd be jacking the story up. Those two hacks would be on the phone to every impotency support group and health professional they could get hold of to read them Watson's comedy turn. About an hour before deadline they would invite the Chief Constable to comment. Scooter had helpfully pointed out that the chief was to be found in the 19th hole at the Royal Leamington golf club between 8pm and 10.30 on weekends.

As expected, Silverside was found guilty. He said nothing. Unexpectedly he only got six years. He still said nothing, but allowed himself a barely perceptible smile. In passing sentence, Judge Grudge-Fortune said it was truly a tragedy that a man of Silverside's ingenuity could not have found a legal outlet for his undoubted ability. In what were to be his final words in a red gown and wig, at least in a court of law, he ordered the building to be cleared as scuffling broke out when angry relatives tried to charge the dock. The Crown Prosecution Service immediately announced it would appeal the sentence, believing it too lenient and alluding to confusion caused by "eccentric behaviour" on the part of the judge. Fuel was added to the fire of public outrage when it was revealed that at the dealers' trial Porker was sent down for two years and the rest of the gang got 18 months.

'A perfect result,' Monk told a puzzled DC Love over their first coupling of whisky and Thelonious on Saturday night.

Pausing to savour a generous sip of Glen Campbell malt, he added: 'For the Sunday Herald, I mean.'

Within a few hours, Monk was able to see if his forecast was correct. He left Mandy Love slumbering in his double bed, having spent the small hours himself dozing on the leather settee. A gesture which owed more to the debilitating effects of a bottle of Scotland's finest than a sudden onset of chivalry.

At 6am he was at Leamington railway station where the Midlands editions of the Sunday papers were due in on the 6.15 from Marylebone. Monk knew the wholesalers well enough to be allowed to plunder the bales for a copy of each on the platform.

The Herald's front page stood out like a nun mooning in St Peter's Square. Watson was pictured waving a beer glass below a huge headline:

FURY AT POLICE CHIEF'S STAND-UP

Top cop Jeremy Watson, who nabbed the Pinky and Perky gang, is facing the sack for hamming it up in the pub as the mastermind was being jailed.

The Chief Superintendent ignored his boss's last orders and entertained drinkers with a string of "vulgar and inappropriate jokes" about a serious medical condition.

Pressure groups campaigning to raise awareness of male impotence said the laughing policeman's performance, calling for the guilty men to be given "a long stretch" and a "hard time" was a flop.

During his 10-minute turn in the pub, the stand-up detective raised laughs at the judge's expense by labelling him "limp wristed" and accused him of handling the gang leader with kid gloves.

Last night the Chief Constable of Warwickshire, who only days before had warned officers not to take the rise out of the victims of the aphrodisiac drug, announced Watson would be suspended pending a full enquiry.

Full story - pages 2 & 3. Profile of the cop they call Ellie, page 40.

Could it get any better? Monk thought to himself, back at his flat savouring the timing of the Sally Army finale. And then it did. Scooter's emails stopped mid-sentence and he was the phone, beside himself with excitement, boasting about an upgrade to first-class for the New York flight and extending his stay to 10 days.

'All courtesy of Kerching, sorry Beijing,' he shouted.

'The Chinese government has given me an absolute belter of a follow-up for Monday's tabloids. They've ordered the zoo to drop the idea of naming new panda cubs Sherlock and Watson, finally cottoning on to the fact that the case has become an international joke.

'They've issued a statement, get this: "The People's republic of China takes a firm stand on drug abuse. It therefore condemns the remarks of a senior British police officer making fun of the Pinky and Perky perpetrators. In doing so he has ridiculed a health condition that we in China take very seriously and have spent many years and countless rhino horns trying to find a remedy for. As a result we shall not be calling the new cubs Sherlock and Watson. To reflect the traditional values of the Chinese people they will take names meaning a Tower of Strength and to thrive and prosper…"

Scooter paused waiting for Monk's reaction. Unusually the detective gave in.

'Come on out with it Scooter, let's have it. What are they?'

This time it was the hack who savoured the moment for a second before announcing with a flourish: 'Dong and Rong.'

4.
She's a killer...Queen

'You met the Queen while you were out walking your dog?'

Marc Mahoney couldn't disguise his delight as he asked the question. His morning had just got a whole lot brighter. What seemed like a standard golden wedding anniversary write-up for the Kenilworth Messenger had moved in his mind's eye from the page opposite the Births, Marriages and Deaths to a contender for the coveted lead story on page three.

'That's what I said, yes. We were exercising Marshall on the public paths behind the castle. He was just a pup then, of course,' Tom Howard replied, patting the head of a slumbering overweight Labrador lying at the slippered feet of his wife.

Cath Howard had been edgy from the moment Mahoney walked through the door of their 1950s semi with veteran snapper Bobby Dole. The photographer's forced cheeriness hadn't worked its usual magic in breaking the ice. Experience told him that Mrs Howard was either fretting about having her picture taken or there was something in their marriage she didn't want to talk about, perhaps the death of a child. He noticed there were no family pictures adorning the walls.

'Tom, are we sure this is the right time? We'll be laughing stock, you know that,' she pleaded, turning to face her husband.

Mahoney feared that the best line in the story was about to disappear and he'd have to fall back on the anniversary formula. The editor's command echoed in his ears: 'Don't forget, ask them the secret of their long and happy marriage.'

Even a junior reporter like Mahoney, who'd only been in the job six months, knew the answer would be either 'give and take,' or 'never go to bed on an argument.'

Tom Howard clutched his wife's left hand tightly and stared at the wedding ring that she had worn every day for 50 years.

'I don't care if they do laugh, love. We know what happened and I always said that one day we should tell our story. Now is that day.'

Mahoney hid his puzzlement over why it should be a laughing matter and nodded encouragingly.

'I can assure you Mrs Howard that our readers will be thrilled to hear how a local couple bumped into the Queen while out with their dog. Was it during an official visit to the town by her majesty, Mr Howard?'

'You might say that. Queen Elizabeth had been attending banquets and carnivals thrown by an admirer in her honour. Elizabeth the First, that is.'

Mahoney's pen froze above his notepad. He turned to his photographer, whose eyes were raised to the ceiling, lips forming a silent oath: 'Nutters.'

She's a Killer .... Queen

'Ha, ha, I see, you're going to tell me it was a historical re-enactment, aren't you?' Mahoney said with a jauntiness he no longer felt.

Dole instinctively chipped in with a lame joke. 'We can put in under the late news column, Mr Howard.

'About 500 years, isn't it, since the Virgin Queen stayed over at Kenilworth Castle?'

'Four hundred and forty-one on July 9, to be precise, for the most famous visit,' Tom Howard replied, adding without a trace of humour, 'and nearly three years since we saw her.'

'I know what you're thinking: "a pair of fruitcakes. Get us out of here." But hear us out, lads. We're not mad; we need to get this off our chests. We don't expect you'll print a word of it. Just listen to our story.'

'I'll get the tea,' Cath said. 'Does everyone have milk?'

'You'd better bring in the pot, Mrs Howard,' chimed in Dole, 'and all the biscuits you can muster.'

Tom popped a sweetener into his china teacup, gave it a resolute stir and began.

'It was the first time we'd let Marshall off the lead, and he did a runner, belting off towards the bumps, as we call them, behind the castle water meadow.

'They always remind me of the Telly Tubby hill. Never knew what they were, just some sort of old earthworks. We thought Marshall had spotted a rabbit, he was barking like mad when we reached him.'

'Then we heard the sobbing,' Cath said. 'A really mournful, heartfelt crying. Down in a grassy hollow a pale woman with copper hair was crouched on her heels, hiding her face in a large handkerchief, like a child might, thinking we couldn't see her. When she revealed her face, pain and anguish were carved into her delicate features like unhealed scars.'

Tom looked uncomfortable and nodded apologetically at his wife's sympathetic description.

'I'm not proud of it, but my first instinct was to scoop up Marshall and clear off. We've got two daughters, grown-up now and both married, but in my experience there's usually one of two reasons for that sort of reaction by a woman: the time of the month or man trouble. If you're unlucky, both.'

Cath shook her head. Mahoney and Dole looked at the floor, embarrassed for her.

'Well as I say, I'm not proud of it. But Cath did the right thing; put an arm around her shoulder and asked if we could help, phone someone to come. Family maybe.'

'That started her sobbing again, more violently,' said Cath. 'She began screaming hysterically, ranting something about her mother losing her head and her father being a murderer.

'That was when I started thinking she might be a psychiatric patient who'd wandered off from the mental health unit at the hospital. It wouldn't have been the first time.

'And she looked, well, eccentric would be putting it kindly. She was wearing a crude earth-coloured dress, like a peasant's robe, with clumpy leather overshoes strapped around silk slippers. No makeup but her skin had a translucent quality. I guessed she was around the forty mark. Not pretty, but with her red ringlets and pale skin she was very striking. Had what I call presence.'

'And then she stopped blubbering and spoke,' Tom added. 'The change was astonishing. She was suddenly composed and in control, voice was clear and cold as ice. It was if we were seeing a different woman from the emotional wreck of seconds before.

'She said we could help her by listening to her confession but we were to say nothing and to go when she finished. Cath, you can remember it better than me. You tell it.'

The Queen's Speech

The common people called me the Virgin Queen. The fools. Sebastian, my handsome captain of the guard would taunt me with it as we romped in my bed chamber on log-fired winter evenings.

Then they would have me as bride-in-waiting for dear Robert, the Earl of Leicester, who panted after me like a doting puppy. My love for him was that for a faithful friend, a companion since childhood, there when needed for comfort like a fireside dog. One never allowed to stray into the bedroom.

I called him The Robin. Like the red-breasted bird, his bright and busy nature amused me. But the robin is a deceptive creature that can use his beak to drill the skull of interlopers when his territory is threatened. I never saw Robin's darker side but I had heard, as everyone did, the stories about his wife's death. I believed his account, convinced he couldn't lie to me about his beloved Amy.

He sobbed as he told me how the surgeons were unable to cut the disease from her breast. How in her weakened state and all hope faded, she'd fallen from the bed when the nurse had left her side to summon the physician.

Robin swore the story, believed by her subjects, from pauper to prince, that he'd pushed her down a staircase, was the work of rumour-mongering political enemies. Secretly, I would admit that I was happy that the rumour persisted and gained purchase, for it meant that it was unthinkable that he should ever propose marriage to me, the Queen of England. For all his wealth, the magnificent Kenilworth Castle and his political power, he could not change public opinion, in whose eyes he was a murderer.

But he could cock a snook at the mob and demonstrate his love for me in another way. For nearly three weeks, I was his exalted guest at the castle and each day he staged increasingly lavish ways to dote. Pageants in my honour were held on this very ground by the most brilliant players in the land. On the mere, a floating island was built to home a mermaid as tall as a knight's charger, sculpted to the finest detail by artists over many months. On a full moon, as the island circled the lake towed by hidden chains, the castle walls flared in rainbow showers, spectacular fireworks that could be seen for miles around,

The very best Italian landscapers were brought over to construct a knot garden for my use alone. It held the rarest plants in the kingdom and beyond. Should I care to walk out by the castle walls, acrobats and jugglers from three countries were standing by along the ramparts to perform, hoping I would glance up and recognise their endeavours.

We feasted every night on banquets that could have fed a hundred peasants for a week on what was left when we retired. Wine was as bountiful as the water in the mere. The guests, the richest and noblest in England together with their counterparts from twenty foreign courts, plunged in readily and took their fill.

On every one of the nineteen days of this sojourn of excess thousands of townsfolk gathered from dawn outside the castle gate, ready to cheer me should I deign to show my face. Even if I did not they were happy exchanging gossip about the comings and goings, delighting in shocking one another with estimates of the costs, which they'd plucked from the air and doubled.

They thought such an extravagant show of affection could only have been countenanced by a lover so besotted he had lost his senses. I admit I had begun to think that too. I accepted that The Robin and I were in many ways meant for each other. As brother and sister. He was my counsel, my rock, a wiser sibling who took the place abdicated by my father. An ally and a devoted friend who indulged me, but never in my eyes a husband.

When I realised the scale of the celebrations and the

fortune he must have sacrificed, I was shocked. This was far, far beyond thumbing his nose at his enemies; this was a declaration to the world that I was the most precious thing in his life. He wanted everyone to know I was the love of his life. But he wasn't mine and far from being swept off my feet by his extravagance I felt trapped, overwhelmed. Like a child who's been given too many presents at Christmas.

By the seventh day I was bloated on rich food, wine and the fawning of Robin and his friends, and took to my bed. I sent for my physician and ordered him to diagnose my condition as a pre-fever malaise for which a day of walking in the fresh-air of the Warwickshire countryside was the best remedy. Despite Robin fussing like an old woman with his dire warnings of the dangers lurking behind every hedgerow I was insistent I should go.

'I am the Queen and I shall do exactly as I please,' I wrote in a note to him after he'd stormed out of my private rooms. 'I shall be accompanied by my personal bodyguard, the captain, and his two best swordsmen. I shall not be recognised as the Queen as my robe will be that of a humble peasant, a hood shall cover my face. The men will be garbed as farm labourers and their weapons hidden. I will leave at dawn and return by dusk. If you have me followed I shall leave the castle and never utter one word to you again.'

A mist was still hanging over the mere as we left the following morn, but the watery sun was showing well-enough to promise enveloping warmth later. The cap-

She's a Killer .... Queen

tain obviously had similar intentions and instructed his two men to follow fifty paces behind, well out of earshot.

Truth be told, there was little to hear that would have given us away as lovers. We talked easily about the excesses of the past few days, tried to best each other by naming the hedgerow flowers and song birds along the way and paused often at the small stream we were following to see if we could spot the sparkle of a trout basking in the shallows. We didn't need anything else. It was just how I had imagined a fledgling romance might be, had I not been born different.

I had suffered many suitors since I came of age. Princes from Denmark, Spain and Sweden; the King of France, all seeking a political union. Their passion was for more power. I was merely a means to that end.

Courtiers from my own land were as numerous as the mayfly hatching along that lonely stream, and would have been as short-lived. For their ardour also would have died after they'd planted their seeds. I did not intend to be the vessel for their vanity. My father chartered that route and is remembered as an overweight ogre who treated his wives as breeding mares

I would not give up a sliver of my power let alone be subjugated by the rule of a man occupying my throne. What I wanted on that day, walking with my compliant lover, was to banish a dark yearning for something else, something that was recognised long ago.

'You are different, like me,' my French governess had whispered in my ear on my 12th birthday, before kissing me tenderly on the lips.

By early afternoon we reached the stream's end as it flowed into a broad river. The four of us sat down on the bank and shared the contents of a hamper prepared by the castle's kitchens. Had any of the passing peasants looked at our fayre they may have wondered how simple folk could afford quails' eggs, huge hams, chicken breasts and a flagon of red wine. The wine and the warm sun soon dulled my senses and as the two soldiers diplomatically excused themselves to scout the route we should take, I fell into the captain's arms and slept deeply, as a baby might encircled by a mother's embrace.

How I wish we had headed back when I awoke. The perfect day, a fleeting taste of what might have been in another lifetime, would have remained in my memory until I drew my final breath. Now it returns to haunt me every waking hour and invades my dreams like a dark shadow gripping my throat.

The two guards returned, not bothering to hide the smirks on their faces, taking my rumpled appearance as evidence that their lusty captain had serviced his queen.

'The river path will take us to Stoneleigh, captain,' said Richard, the bigger of the two.

'There's a smithy there and I dare say the farrier would welcome the feel of an unexpected sovereign in exchange for a mount.'

I would have let his bawdy puns pass as I wanted nothing to spoil my day. But the captain struck him with a fearsome blow and drew his dagger to the soldier's throat, drawing a crimson trickle.

'You will hold your tongue, Sir. Hold it in your hand

along with your eyes and ears if you dare to make jests again. Lead the way to Stoneleigh and thank god that you still have breath to do so.'

The mood darkened after that. The playful stream was now a turbulent river, deep and brooding, dangerous. We made our way warily, unsure of our footing. The sun had lost its warmth.

As we descended a steep hill into the riverside hamlet we were welcomed by the sounds of merry ballads and laughter. Alongside the old church a field was decked in bunting and sagging long tables were laden with wedding foods. Families were tucking in gratefully.

A quenelle was underway at the far end of the field and we could see strapping farm lads charging at the wooden figures, their lumbering cart horses struggling to keep a line as the riders' crude lances were lowered with deadly intent, hoping beyond reason for a clean strike.

The beating hearts of the festivities were beneath a large oak bearing a rope swing threaded with flowers. It cradled the bride and groom, looking as happy as I had been earlier in the day. I felt a pang of envy that stopped my breath. This was their day and they could look forward to many others. They would have children, grow old together, probably end their lives in this same village and be buried alongside this church.

At that moment, though I was envious I was also happy for them. I wanted to get closer to feel their glow, hoping some might stay with me as a lucky omen. I meant no malice then.

'Stay here while I continue alone,' I ordered the captain and his men while we were still shielded by the church from view. 'You will arouse suspicion. I am going to offer my blessing to the bride and give her a small gift.'

As I walked past the guests, what had been raucous banter suddenly quietened, the tussles among ruddy-faced children stopped. Faces turned to me with questioning stares: 'Who is she? Where is she from? Why does she shield her face?'

Too late I realised my stupidity. In this isolated hamlet any stranger would be seen as a threat. This was a place where everyone's business was common knowledge; they shared the same surnames, worked alongside each other in the fields. A newcomer was to be feared.

A lone robin watched me from the tree as I hastened my step, giving the wary hosts little chance to see beneath my tightly drawn hood. Those who did catch a glimpse would have seen a fixed smile and trickling sweat running down my throat.

The bride was called Eppie. She was no more than seventeen, hair golden as the ripening corn, eyes the hue of flecked hazel shells. Her bridal gown, crudely stitched of rough linen, far from detracting from her beauty, provided a plain palette on which it could sparkle unopposed.

As I approached, her pale lips quivered and those soft brown eyes darted, afraid to meet my captivated gaze. She was looking for a saviour. The broad-shouldered boy, for that's all he was, put his plough-muscled arm around her, gamely protecting his wife of little more than an hour. He challenged me to state my business, but a quiver in his voice exposed his fear.

'I bring you only good wishes and a small gift,' I said, aware of the murmurings gathering behind me. I slipped off a ring from my little finger, one that Robin had given me. To me it was a trifling thing, a poesy ring made of gold and rock crystal with an inscription in Latin which I hadn't bothered to read.

To that village girl it must have seemed as if the planets had dropped it on her palm. But, unworldly as she was, she had a fiery pride. She looked at her wedding ring, a roughly fashioned band of pewter, and thrust the poesy back at me.

'I have a ring, please take this and leave. I have no need of your gift.'

Many subjects had lost their tongues for less. But in my shocked hesitation, her maid of honour grabbed the ring, saw the strange words of inscription and dropped it like a burning ember.

'The devil's words, a witch is among us,' she screamed.

The chant 'witch, witch, witch' took hold of the mob who'd padded forward like stealthy wolves. Their baying raised the vicar from his wine-induced slumber in the nave and he burst out into the light, holding aloft a gold cross and began reciting the Lord's Prayer. It acted as a signal for the pack to pounce. I was struck to the head and fell heavily to the ground. Hands clawed at my hood but I had it clutched tightly still.

Some of my face must have shown because I could

hear the fool of a vicar exclaim: 'She has the red hair of the devil's messenger and the paleness of a ghost,' as I was dragged towards the river bank.

Had it not been for Sebastian and his men reacting so swiftly, my last taste of life would have been the slime of the river bed filling my throat. But it was the iron taste of red blood that splattered my lips as I lay in the dirt. The life of two villagers draining on me as they clutched their throats, severed by the soldiers' blades.

The three protectors stood over me, forming a lethal triumvirate, soldiers against toothless curs.

'Who struck the blow to this woman,' the captain demanded, moving his stare to each in turn of the quivering men. No answer came and he turned to look at me. I wish I could say that in my anger and distress I was confused and unable to know my own mind. But I was not. In a moment of absolute clarity and intent I looked straight at the groom and pointed him out.

'It was he.'

He had no time to protest his innocence. His handsome head was rolling down the river bank before the captain's sword had finished its deadly arc. His bride, now his widow, threw herself after it but was held back by the vicar and those men not frozen in fear at the events they had witnessed.

I was hauled across the captain's shoulder like a bale of straw and we ran to the far end of the field. We made off on the same horses which earlier we had witnessed carrying vibrant young men celebrating their friend's betrothal. Now they were making good the escape of his executioners.

When we reached the brow of the hill, we stopped and looked back on the village I had ripped the heart from. The two soldiers looked down with sad eyes, but when they glanced at me I could see contempt. They must have seen me felled and knew it couldn't have been the groom, who was seated.

I took the captain to one side out of their hearing. He nodded gravely as I whispered my commands to him. When we left that sad place, there was only us two riding away. In the days that followed, the stiffened corpses of two naked men would be found by the villagers, propped either side of a stout oak, their chests gashed with a cross of congealed blood.

The discovery comforted the tight community of Stoneleigh. The devil had turned on his own became their new mantra.

They were right. I had turned on the captain, forcing him to obey his queen. The execution of his men marked the death of any affection there was between us. He had seen me for what I was: my father's daughter. A killer queen. It was in my blood.

He knew more than any man that I was harbouring a dark secret, the reason why I had never given myself fully to him.

As we neared the castle, he confronted me with a question to which he knew the answer. They were the last words that passed between us. 'Why did you choose the groom?'

I rode on in silence but to myself I allowed my inner

voice to speak openly. I was insanely jealous, it said. The groom had the prize I most desired.

The living room in the Howards' semi was as silent as the grave as Cath Howard finished her retelling of the Queen's speech.

Bobby Dole was speechless for once. However fantastical the story, whoever they had met on that walk, he was certain the Howards were sincere. They believed they had encountered the Queen.

Tom Howard was still staring into his tea-cup. Beyond caring whether they had been convinced. He could have added further evidence, pointed out that he shared the name of Queen Elizabeth's maternal grandfather. It may hold the key to why they had been chosen to hear the Queen's confession. But he kept that to himself. If the reporter and photographer were not persuaded by now, it would not sway them. The silence had become oppressive.

And so it fell to the gauche Mahoney to break the black spell that hung over the gathering.

'So, Mr and Mrs Howard, what do you think is the secret of your long and happy marriage?'

5.
Ballad of Jim and Oscar

MIDSUMMER'S Day in a Paris that is failing to live up to its billing as La Ville-Lumière. The city of light is overcast, offering visitors an afternoon matinee of grey clouds and drizzle. Take it or leave it. Waiters at the pavement cafes clustered around the Gare du Nord share the sentiment, whatever the weather. Nevertheless they are preparing for a rush. For they can hear the station's scratchy tannoys blaring out the arrival of the 4pm Eurostar from London, simultaneously in French and English. The hopelessly entangled announcements dissipate into the indifference of the disembarking clatter of passengers, only for the void to be filled by a North American voice pleading in Franglais with a station master.

'Peer...Le Chase, Peer...Le...Chase. Mort, mort...Ou est le metro de mort? Mort...mort, metro mort. Pour la cite des morts...' The tourist is shouting, arms aloft in despair at the official's inability to understand his own language.

'Monsieur, Je ne comprends pas. I. Do. Not. Understand. Okay. We do not have dead railway stations. Are you feeling a little unwell, too many beers, perhaps? You need to please move on.'

Lizzie Chace, who's just stepped off the train, gamely butts in to help, regardless of the fact that her French oral barely scraped a pass at GCSE. Had there been an exam in tact she would have got an F.

'Pardon, Monsieur, I think this man is trying to get to Père Lachaise cemetery, known as the "City of the dead." He's not drunk, just American.'

'Ah, Americain, Je comprise. Mort! Metro!' The station official's delight is not shared by the irate passenger.

'That's an outrageous thing to say.'

'What, drunk?'

'No, American.'

'Sorry, didn't think you Yanks were so sensitive.'

'They may not be. But we Canadians are. You know, Canada, big place, Mounties, lumberjacks - you come to it when you get to Uncle Sam's ceiling. We are in the loft.'

'Canadian, then. Same thing. Fewer McDonald's, more trees. And didn't the Yanks spoil your rear view by moving into Alaska?'

'And where would you be from, Miss Diplomacy?'

'Not that it's any of your business, but I was brought up in Somerset in the West Country.'

'Yeah, I've heard about it. Same as Wales, right? Only not as many sheep.'

Touché!' Lizzie concedes, acknowledging with an

appraising raised eyebrow an impasse in the flirting foreplay.

They both feel a spark between them, but which one of them is going to take it past the silly jousting stage? Lizzie waits for a lead-in that doesn't come. In what is tantamount to surrender, she says she knows where they can catch the best Tube for Père Lachaise. It's where she was heading before preventing him being arrested for abuse of the French language, ha, ha. Lizzie Chace, by the way, now of London, on a budget break and hoping to get to the cemetery to visit the grave of Oscar Wilde before the gates shut.

The tanned face now smiling at her is trying hard not to look smug at having won the first round. But he can't resist noting his small victory. 'If that's an invitation, Rich Hunter accepts. That's my name, by the way, not my occupation.'

He's a musician in Vancouver taking a vacation with his buddies. Make those ex-buddies. They got wasted last night in a sleazy bar in Soho and are doing their own impression of a city of the dead in the hotel, leaving Billy-no-buddies to catch the Eurostar solo.

Rich notices Lizzie's left hand is ringless. Can't fail to really as she's waving it in front of him, clutching a copy of The Rough Guide to Dead Places, saying it advises visitors to ignore the main Metro line to Père Lachaise station and take an alternative route to Gambetta, the closest to the cemetery entrance for Oscar Wilde's grave. She spots a dingy white-tiled tunnel that looks like an abandoned public toilet, circa 1900.

'That must be it, probably part of the old station, but I can't see any sign on it. Which fits with the French policy of confusing the enemy, particularly the English. It's a backdoor they would rather keep to themselves by disguising it as an Edwardian pissoir's back passage. Accounts for why we seem to be the only visitors prepared to chance it for a trip to Père Lachaise on a grey midsummer's night. Where's their spirit of adventure? It's not as though you hope for sunshine in a cemetery. Twilight, a light drizzle; a melancholy mist perhaps, the air heavy with the overbearing sadness of greatness dripping from hanging moss and crumbling marble.'

'You're a writer, then?'

'What makes you say that?'

'Just a wild guess.'

'Well not a writer, as in novelist. On-line news journalist for the Herald. Strikeout journalist. More caption writer for pics of bums, boobs, bikinis – so long as they're attached to celebrities. Strikeout news; question mark celebs. Today I'm a wannabe writer seeking inspiration for a Gothic tale at the grave of Oscar Wilde. We can all dream, especially tonight. What about you?'

'What about me?'

'What you do, what sort of music?'

'Any sort. Rock and jazz mainly. I'm a freelance studio engineer who plays a bit of rhythm guitar when they can't get anyone better.'

'So you don't perform, then?'

'Er, we've got a little fun band together to bring in extra

Ballad of Jim and Oscar

bucks. Sort of tribute act, a send-up but we have a good time.'

'And...?'

'And, that's it, sorry to disappoint.'

'Who's the tribute to..? You don't have the hair for Shania Twain and please don't tell me it's Michael Bublé.'

'Think of the Boss and Benny; Springsteen meets ABBA, and what've you got?'

'I dread to think.'

'Bjorn to Run! The band that serves the ultimate rock and pop smorgasbord.'

'You're making it up.'

'Hey, don't knock it. Those gigs pay for trips like this, besides I enjoy it. You'd be surprised how well some of those songs mesh. Changing the subject: Oscar Wilde? Wasn't he that floppy-haired Irish guy who got banged up for buggery?'

'You got it in one. Some might argue he was the greatest wit, raconteur and playwright of the 19th century, martyred for his bi-sexuality and an enduring icon for gay rights. But floppy-haired Irish guy banged up for buggery cuts to the chase. Ever thought of being a journalist?'

'You're not one of those sad people that plants a lipstick kiss on his gravestone, are you?' Rich asks, enjoying provoking her.

'For someone who can't even pronounce the name of the cemetery you seem to know an awful lot of the customs. And no, I'm not one of those sad people. But whose grave are you visiting among the great and gone at Père Lachaise? Let me think. Chopin, Proust, Molière maybe? Give me a clue.'

'Okay,' he says, ignoring the sarcasm, and sings:

Riders on the storm, riders on the storm,
Into the world we're born, into this world we're torn....'

'Not Chopin, then. Give me another clue.'

'Leather trousers… lady killer.'

'Will Young! No damn it. Not dead, definitely not a lady killer but probably has a pair of leather pants. One last clue.'

'He left this life early Doors; helped on his way by his best friend Jack Daniels and substances in keeping with the life of a rock god and poet.

'Jim Morrison! American pop singer, nice hair, prone to over exposure on stage.'

'Got it in three,' says Rich in mock surprise. 'I'd have put more weight on writer than singer and he was not a flasher. It was what papers like yours would call a wardrobe malfunction. He was tucking in his shirt while exhorting the crowd to revolution.'

'Must have been another Jim Morrison who was sentenced for indecent exposure during a concert, then. Are you one of those sad fans who leave a glass of Jack Daniels at his graveside?'

'Pardon.'

'Must have been another…'

'No. Pardoned. Morrison was later pardoned by the court. And even If you're right about the subway sign, it still seems odd that we are the only ones in Paris taking your route.'

'I've done my homework. While your fellow Americans, sorry Canadians, and the rest of the tourist hordes go to Père Lachaise or Philippe Auguste stations, we'll be taking a shortcut that'll get us to the tomb of Oscar Wilde, leaving just enough daylight for me to take a few pictures and ponder the tragedy of a misunderstood genius. While you, presumably, will stumble around looking for the grave decorated with crude graffiti and sad tumblers of Jack Daniels. Did you bring a glass, by the way, or were you going to leave the bottle for Jim?'

They walk off towards the tunnel, each believing they had established early supremacy. Their footsteps echo in the mouth of the entrance as they approach; the joyful sound of an accordion drifts out to greet them. The tune is from the musical Gigi. Thank Heaven for Little Girls. The busker is a fragile old lady with wispy ginger hair. She has placed a black shawl at her feet, which are shod in old sandals, and plays with an exuberance that belies her wasted appearance, remembering perhaps that she once had the world at her feet.

'Well, we're not entirely alone. Looks like we have a busker to guide us,' Lizzie says. 'Poor old dear, she's wearing sandals. It's freezing down here. I'm going to give her my change.

'Madame, you play beautifully. I am a big fan of Gigi and that is my favourite song.'

As she stoops to place the coins on the shawl, the old lady takes her hands off the accordion and cups Lizzie's startled face sensuously.

'Permit me, my English Rose, to show my gratitude with a kiss to your velvet cheek.'

'Of course, when in Paris and all that do as the Romans do. Ha, ha.'

'Ma chérie, the Romans boast of many things but in my experience spend too much time talking about what they will do and not living up to expectations. My Italian lovers were like their Coliseum, not as big as I imagined and no longer able to put on much of a show.'

'All mouth and no trousers, as we English might say,' Lizzie says. 'Merci Madame, you have a very gentle touch … on the accordion I mean, not erm…'

'Ah, my English rose, you blush. Such a delicate bloom. You may need to grow thorns to protect yourself from predators. I wish I had known that when I was your age, my dear. It would have stopped Willy climbing all over me.'

'Yes, well, moving on,' Rich interjects. 'We have a train to catch. So sorry to hear about your Willy, they can grow rampantly in a sultry climate if you don't cut them back.'

'Willy was my first husband, Monsieur. An ugly overweight professional charlatan who nevertheless was as determined and surefooted as an old goat when it came to negotiating the terrain of a woman's body and finding his way into her heart. Perhaps it was because he didn't have one himself he captured so many. I can forgive him that as I too was a collector. But the fat pig also stole my early books, passed them off as his own work, basking in what should have been my glory, rolling

Ballad of Jim and Oscar 97

in my money. Be on your guard against the Willies of this world, English Rose.'

The old lady shifts her gaze, accusingly, to Rich, before returning to smile at Lizzie. She starts to play again the famous song from Gigi, this time bursting into song *Thank heaven for little girls ....*

She continues to hum the melody as the beguiled couple move a few paces away, believing the old lady is in a world of her own making.

'Well, my fragrant rose,' Rich teases, 'I guess one of us is welcome in very Gay Paree. Thank heaven she hasn't got a pair of shears attached to that accordion. I get the distinct feeling I would be taking a pruning on behalf of Willy.'

'I shouldn't take it personally, you and half the population would qualify,' Lizzie says, distractedly.

Elizabeth Chace may not have excelled in French at school but she was an A-streamer when it came to musicals, especially Gigi. Especially its stage star, Audrey Hepburn. What school girl didn't want to look like her? Though not as a Gigi, perhaps, which even in Lizzie's adolescence had become un-PC, telling as did of a young girl being groomed to be a courtesan (French euphemism for a toff's high-end prostitute, as her drama teacher once memorably dismissed it) It was based on a novella by Colette. An author certainly not on the exam syllabus. Lizzie recalled reading that Colette was responsible for the then unknown Hepburn getting the title role on stage after spotting her in a Monte Carlo hotel and insisting to the director: 'I have found Gigi.'

She also remembered how the sixth-form girls passed around a dog-eared biography of the famous writer. The most racy passages, and there were many, marked by furtive adolescent thumb prints. They'd all sniggered when they read that Colette's first lover, before she was famous, went by the ridiculous, but appropriate, pen name of Willy. The only reason she wasn't famous by that time was that Henry Gauthier-Villars, to give him his real name, ripped off her bodice, married her, and then ripped off her first novels, publishing them as his own work. She went on to outshine him in just about everything. More promiscuous, with men and women, more outrageous when it came to shocking polite Paris society. More revealing, in every sense, not least in her celebrated burlesque performances, and without doubt a more talented and prolific writer, credited with some of the most popular novels in 20th century French literature. Her legendary status, though indestructible, didn't protect her wealth or health. Crippled with arthritis and dressed in pauper's hand-me-downs, she cut a sorry figure slumped on Paris streets in the years before her death in 1954, aged 81. Her friends paid for her to be buried at Père Lachaise.

Lizzie paused respectfully as she finished telling all this to Rich, expecting him to be stunned by its implications, if not teary-eyed at the pathos.

'Didn't she also give her name to the skirt that's split up the middle like a pair of shorts?' he asked.

Ballad of Jim and Oscar

'Ha, bloody ha. You're such a wise guy. But I'll bet even you have watched Gigi on the TV sometime. Hello? Maurice Chevalier? Thank Heaven for Little Girls? Our busker thinks she is Colette.'

The old lady has stopped playing and has heard every word of the exchange.

'Not bad, my English rose. You are better informed than your American friend. Perhaps. He makes a poor joke to cover his embarrassment but I suspect he knows more than he lets on. Or maybe he is jealous of our, how would you put it, our Brief Encounter? I did not have a hand in the culottes, although I may wish I had. In France the word is most used to refer to an item of a woman's underwear, or lack of it. As in …'

'Sans culottes,' Rich interrupts. 'As in going commando. And I am not American!'

'Voila! Our Not-Americain is not as naive as he pretends to be.'

'How on earth did you know that?' Lizzie asks.

'Must've read it on the InFlight magazine on the plane.'

'Monsieur Not-Americain, I have found to my cost that many men are natural liars. You however should never play poker unless you want to leave the table without your shirt. It is possible that you are not as stupid as you would like us to believe. We shall see when I accompany you to what, as your beautiful companion has noted is my terminus, Père Lachaise.'

'No. Really that won't be necessary, though it's really most kind of you' Lizzie says.

'Mademoiselle, let me be clear. I will be your

companion on our train fantome. If I may risk a pun you English are so fond of, without me you would not have a ghost of a chance of being allowed on. Your spirit has got you this far, but without tickets your adventure is over, dead and buried. Now, please look on the back of this ticket and scratch off the square of foil. You will see a small picture.'

'Two plums?'

'Exactement! You, Monsieur Not-Americain, must present this second ticket to the guard. But you must not remove the foil.'

Rich protests, saying they will take their chances and pay on board, but gives in after Lizzie kicks his ankle and takes him aside. Her imagination has got the better of her early fears. Besides, she has dealt with bigger crazies than this harmless old lady every day on the Northern Line. She admits to Rich she is captivated by her story. Brief Encounter? Train Fantome? Scratch card tickets! It's either an elaborate reality TV hoax, or they are guinea-pigs for the French tourist board's pilot video of The Lachaise Experience. Ideas courtesy of the Magic Kingdom, Willy Wonka and historical re-enactments. They agree to play along.

The tired chugging of a petrol engine gasping in the tunnel precedes the arrival of a single carriage being helped to the platform by a centenarian train. Together they had witnessed the opening of the Metro and, like proud war vets, wear their scars openly like medals. The livery is battered and faded but the pioneering spirit remains.

The moustachioed guard is standing on the footplate, bristling with self-importance and brandishing a megaphone. He addresses the three figures on the platform as if they were a crowd.

'Special service to Père Lachaise. Tickets must be ready for inspection. No cash, credit cards or special pleadings accepted. And I reserve the right to refuse anyone who isn't French, particularly Americans and English. Ah, Madame Colette, forgive me for not recognising you. It has been many years, please step aboard. You others step away from the train, you have the wrong platform.'

'No, wait, please, I have a ticket… un billet! Here, look…' Lizzie shouts.

'Un Billet? And deux prunes, I see. Bon. But not bon enough and you are English if I am not mistaken.'

'Almost Welsh really, give or take a few sheep and a bit of water. And my friend - who is not American - has the second ticket.'

Rich decides to go on the attack: 'Greetings from La Belle Canada, French cousin. Quebec sends a big 'Salut!' The rest of the country says a big howdy (there's an embarrassing silence as his attempt at a joke falls flat) …er, here's my ticket, guard.'

'We shall see what is revealed… A hammer! Monsieur, I must have a third plum. This is not a match.'

'You are mistaken,' says Colette. 'A hammer is more than a match for two plums. It is my little joke, now step aside, Monsieur, this couple are my special guests. Come, we will sit at the front facing our fellow passengers. The show is about to begin. I have arranged a little welcome for you.'

The carriage doors open. Inside, twelve couples are seated, dressed as if characters from a painting by Lautrec of the audience at the Moulin Rouge. The men have shiny top hats and are heavily bearded; their mistresses are dressed for a night at the theatre. They all stare fixedly ahead. The carriage lights dim and as the old train lowers its rhythmic beat, a tiny birdlike woman rises from her seat and stands commandingly in the centre of the carriage. Colette plays the introduction to La Vie en Rose on her accordion. The singer's tiny stature gives no clue to the raw power of emotion it contains when she sings of her lover's overwhelming magical spell.

The voice could have held a grand theatre spellbound, let alone a train carriage audience. Rich is the first to break the silence. 'What the hell,' he mutters, louder than he intended.

Colette glares at him, lifting her hand away from the keys to stab an accusing finger.

'Au contraire, Monsieur Not-Americain, you should look higher than hell for such a heavenly voice, that of the Little Sparrow.'

'Edith Piaf, another one of Père Lachaise's celebrity residents, who died in 1963,' Lizzie says, entranced by the performance.

'Correct again, English rose. Edith, my good neighbour who moved in nine years after me.'

'Look, I know who it is,' Rich says. 'Or at least I know

the song, but why is it being sung on this train? What's with the fancy dress party? I haven't been so spooked on the underground since I heard Mind the Gap on the Tube for the first time.'

'I don't know anymore,' Lizzie admits. 'If it's some off-the-wall tourism pitch then they've certainly outshone Disney's welcome and put Mickey in the shade. But why just us? Perhaps Madame Colette can enlighten u...'

Before she can finish, their busker companion has lifted her accordion and struck the opening chords of Piaf's famous anthem: *Je Ne Regrette Rien*. The Little Sparrow's voice fills every nook and cranny of the old carriage with unanswerable defiance.

At the last rousing verse, the passengers stand and sing along with gusto, stopping only to let the star finish on the final lingering note. There is a moment's silence before the guard, who has been standing silently on the footplate, raises his megaphone and turns inward to deliver a public announcement to an open-mouthed Lizzie and Rich.

'Attention, Mademoiselle and Monsieur. The guardians of Père Lachaise hope you have *no regrets* about your visit.

'Be warned that taking souvenirs from the cemetery is strictly forbidden. You leave only with your memories not memorials.

'Sadly I have to inform you that there has been a gross act of vandalism at the tomb of Monsieur Oscar Wilde. His testicles have been removed.

'That is, broken off the erotic winged messenger carved by the famous sculptor Jacob Epstein.

Be on your guard if you are offered a round stone the size of a melon as a paperweight. Ask if it is one of a pair and if the answer is yes, you should report it to the police immediately.

'They were believed to have been broken off and carried away by two English women who took exception to their size.

'Perhaps it should not be so surprising that the English were behind such an outrage. I understand they have a Monsieur Elgin who stole marbles from Greece.

'My apologies Madame Colette, but I am allowed a little joke, too, am I not?'

'That's beyond weird,' Lizzie gasps.

'Beyond weird? Noooo.' Rich says, sarcastically. 'Must happen every day. Tourists warned by a wise-cracking train guard about buying stone testicles from a grave memorial.'

'What's really creeping me out is that it's all true,' Liz says. 'The sculpture caused uproar when it was unveiled, Even the French were shocked. The bohemians had a ball, so to speak, at their prudity. Suggestions that there should be a large fig leaf covering up the offending appendages only added to the ridicule they had to endure. But that all died down, until the castration. What's really strange is that it happened 50 years after the memorial was unveiled. And that was about 1960. In other words, the guard is warning us about something that happened more than half a century ago as if it were

Ballad of Jim and Oscar

last week.'

'That's the French for you,' Rich says. 'Always likely to bear a grudge, especially if the English are involved.'

The train slows then brakes abruptly, jolting the passengers, two of whom lose their shiny top hats. No-one moves to pick them up. Rich is about to retrieve them when the carriage lights dim. He and Lizzie move across to a window and gaze out on a decrepit station, lit by a single gas lamp.

'What happened to the lights?' Lizzie shouts. 'This can't be it; I can't even make out the platform.'

'Look again,' says Rich who's looking out the other side. 'Under that guy's feet. Can't miss him. He's wearing a hooped shirt and holding a torch to his face. Scary white make-up, floppy hat. He looks like one of those street performers you have in Covent Garden. Could be the grown up son of Sideshow Bob and Kate Bush.'

'Jesus, it's Bip'. Lizzie's voice has risen an octave.

'The first name I recognise. But you'll have to help me out with Bip. Does he usually hang around a dark metro doing what looks like a moonwalk in black tights?'

'Bip the Clown. Marcel Marceau's most famous character.'

'Marcel who?

'The world's best-known mime artist; though obviously not in Vancouver. He died in 2007 and...'

'Don't tell me. Was he buried in Peer Le Chase, by any chance?

'Yes. Look he wants us to follow him.'

'I don't know how you were brought up but I was

taught to beware men wearing makeup and panty-hose who try to lure you into a dark passage.'

'It's part of the show, isn't it? A Bip to guide you to the cemetery. The moonwalk is for you Americ... North Americans. A nod to Michael Jackson to make you feel at home. Look, I don't know why we've been chosen but this is some elaborate Gallic Goth's Midsummer Night's Dream played out in street theatre. We've been thrown in as a sort of makeshift Brad and Janet, on loan from Rocky Horror.'

'Of course, silly me, must happen all the time,' Rich replies, 'I should have known. Hey, Bip, cool moonwalk but how about both hands on the torch.'

'Don't think you're going to get a response from a mime artist. No, hang on, I'm wrong, he's poking his middle finger in the air. How rude, and how un-French. Whatever happened to the Gallic shrug? No, wait he's curling his finger round and pointing to the tunnel. He wants us to follow him.'

Bip spins on his heel, picking up the throbbing rhythm of the train's engine. Hands on knees, he moves backwards sashaying from side to side, edging along the narrow platform. The passengers rise as if in a trance. Keeping time with Bip, they step like robots, swinging out their left legs, pause, follow with the right, staying in single file like children crocodiling behind teacher at a school for zombies.

Lizzie and Rich are frozen by the spectacle, only breaking out of their stupor as the snaking line starts to

Ballad of Jim and Oscar

disappear in the darkness. With Bip's whiteface no longer even a dot, they rush to catch up. Too late. They have gone. No choice but to press on into the pitch black, until their feet hit a flight of steps. Above them they can see silhouettes of formidable granite crosses framed by the grey Paris sky.

What little breath they have left between them is quickly lost in a joint gasp of astonishment as they emerge into a crescent of graves. The tombstones stand like the pillars of a decaying amphitheatre, resigned to being the supporting cast to the star holding centre stage. Oscar Wilde's tomb is faced with a massive Sphinx-like flying 'demon-angel' - an Art Deco giant which has gatecrashed a Victorian wake for classicism. It is lit by scores of sentinel candles which cause the day's red lipstick kisses to glisten on the protective glass screen, mocking the silent prudes.

There is no sign of Colette and the other passengers, but they can hear the voices of two men arguing. Instinctively Rich and Lizzie clinch together and take cover behind a towering headstone.

The exchanges get angrier as the two men step into the glow, and turn to face the demon-angel's lap, scene of the crime and numerous violent verbal battles since.

They couldn't be more different. One is wearing leather trousers and an unbuttoned white shirt. A handsome gypsy, feral, wild unkempt hair tumbling in black curls to his shoulders. The other man is a dandy. His hair hangs like curtains, parted with vain precision from the crown and shared equally across his powdered brow. He wears a foppish cravat and a dark frock coat. His mannered elegance would be at war with the other man's coarse beauty had they never exchanged a word. But it was clear they had, many times

'For the last time, Wilde, I did not take your bloody balls. Christ's sake I wasn't even here then, and if I had been I couldn't have cared less. Let it lie, man. It wasn't me.'

'Let us consider the evidence, Morrison. Count one: You are American. The only country that went from barbarism to decadence without civilisation in between. You, Mr Lizard King, have been caught with your pants down. And not for the first time, from what I read.'

'Whoa, dangerous ground, Wilde. At least I had pants on long enough to pull down. And as for being American, only part guilty. The parts that got me into trouble I put down to my Irish ancestors. What was your excuse Mr Oscar Fingal O'Flahertie Wilde?'

'The fact remains, Morrison, your leather-trousered figure was seen crouching by my memorial in the dead of the night. I suggest that jealousy got the better of you and you symbolically neutered me. I must present a constant reminder of your inadequacy. Didn't you once say: "Death makes angels of us all and gives us wings where we had shoulders as smooth as raven's claws?" An entirely mortal line that mocked your pretensions to poetry. You also said some of your worst mistakes in life had been haircuts. If only, Morrison, if only.'

'That was a throwaway remark, Wilde, as you well

know. You've had enough practice yourself. Who was it who said: "When a man is tired of London, he's tired of life?"

I know, the guy standing in front of me, in Paris.'

'The dead man standing in front of you, Morrison. Once a man is tired of life it matters not where he retires. But enough, the fact remains that I represent to you all the sins you never had the courage to commit.'

'I get it, Wilde, when a man is tired of logic, he digs up his old glib quotations. Well, here's one you'll be familiar with: "Arguments are to be avoided, they are always vulgar and often convincing..." Once and for all: I. Didn't. Do. It.'

'Let us call a temporary truce, Morrison. We are both in the gutter, but one of us is still looking at the stars. We have work to do.'

'No need for a truce. I surrender; just don't give me any more of those crap quotations. Look, we've got a day to come up with an act that will show the intellectual hierarchy in this dead and alive hole that we deserve our plots. We are regarded as the foreign interlopers who snuck in under the gate of high art. This concert they propose is for the glorification of themselves, the crème-de-la-crème of French composers, writers, playwrights, dah, dah, de fucking dah. We, Wilde, are no more to them than buskers outside the theatre, not even worthy of a warm-up spot on their stage.'

'For once, what you say may be true. But only of yourself, Morrison. My misfortune is to have been lumped together with you on the grounds that you are

American and they think I am English. Two nations separated by a common...'

'Stop! Your own sayings are bad enough; spare me the ramblings of that other Irish smart-arse.'

'I think you will find that Mr Bernard Shaw stole it from me, Morrison and I prefer the term clever dick rather than smart-arse although they should never be put together, as I found to my cost. I was going on to say, the real reason we are hated is because our adoring, though rather common, followers are a constant reminder of our enduring popularity. Whoever coined the phrase Art for Art's sake, and it may have been me, was wrong. Art for our own sake is what we crave. Personal adulation, Morrison, even if it is expressed in bottles of whisky left at your grave or lipstick kisses on mine.'

'Wilde, I've already told you what we should do at the concert; we blow them away with raw rock, rip open their senses till they see only us, hear us, smell us, reach out and grab us, taste the sweat and spittle flying off us. Get them out of their intellectual little prisons... it'll be like sex.

'And what am I supposed to be doing during this intercourse? No, don't bother to tell me, Morrison. At best the voyeur peeping round the bedroom door, the symbolic post-coital cigarette, humming a verse or two from one of your songs. Perhaps *This is the end my friend*? Your appeal to their base instincts will only feed their snobbery. We are their shackled bear, prodded to dance. My idea is to aim a little higher than their libidos and seek out the narrow cerebral inlet to minds sealed by fossilised bigotry. We shall read one of my plays, sharing the parts. That'll wipe the condescending smiles off their faces.

'How about A Woman of No Importance? They say, Lady Hunstanton, that when good Americans die they go to Paris.

'Indeed, and when bad Americans die, where do they go?'

'Oh, they go to America.'

'For Christ's sake, Wilde, let it go, We either get it together or continue to get cold-shouldered like two dead-beats – which I guess we are in a way.'

The two men fall silent, realising their argument has gone full circle, achieving nothing. They stare at each other, for once lost for words. Rich and Lizzie however are not.

'If this is a tourist come-on Lizzie, it's the most high risk opening that I've seen since the start of the London Olympics. What do these guys think they are doing?'

'Be quiet, they can hear you.'

'Hear me? I don't think they know anything else exists, they're so busy arguing. You could run through the cemetery naked and they wouldn't notice.'

'Thanks for that. Look, I've got an idea. How well do you know Riders on the Storm?'

'Come-on, every half-comatose karaoke rockstar-wannabe in the world knows it.'

'Okay, keep that half a brain active then and look at this poem.' She takes out a small book of Oscar Wilde's poetry from her handbag and opens it at the first page, headed The Ballad of Reading Gaol. Rich peers over, apparently confused by the title.

'The Ballad of Reeding Goal?'

'Reading Gaol, idiot. Wilde's most famous poem, written as you would say after being banged up.'

'So that's what you have tucked away with the lipstick. Every woman hides the thing she loves, eh? Better than killing it, I suppose.'

'You know it! You bastard. You've been stringing me along all the time. "Yet each man kills the things he Loves," Wilde's best-known line. Why the charade?'

'Well, ma'am, us folk from the colonies don't like to spoil the fun you sophisticated people from the old country have in putting us in our place. Yes, I know the poem line by line and I can guess what you're thinking. It's a fit. Morrison's *Riders on the Storm* segued into *The Ballad of Reading Gaol.*'

'It's the line of Wilde's that links it,' Lizzie says: 'the one about two doomed ships that pass in a storm.'

Rich looks at the poem, starts talking through the verses to himself, finding the rhythm easily and then steps from behind the headstone to sing: *'Into this world we're born, into this world we're torn... Riders on the storm.'*

Wilde and Morrison turn to face him, unsurprised, as if they had been expecting guests.

The longest day's light has departed early, ushered away by the dark clouds that have gathered across the city. Wilde and Morrison are poised at either end of the demon-angel sculpture, ready to perform. The

Ballad of Jim and Oscar

passengers from the train are seated in a semicircle in front of them, silent as the grave. A topiaried box hedge defines the wings of the stage, pruned with a line of globes the size of footballs, each bearing a lit candle. The threatened downpour has started its descent some miles away, but announces its impending arrival at Père Lachaise with a roll of thunder; serving as a melodramatic prelude to the Doors' hit. Colette tip taps the ivory keys of her accordion, mimicking the patter of rain, slipping seamlessly into the brooding motif of the song, full and menacing to underpin Wilde's spoken verses, lighter behind Morrison's rich bass voice. The performance begins with Wilde's stentorious delivery taking command of the opening verse. Morrison sings the alternate verses slowly, hardly any faster than Wilde, but all the more effective as a soft counterpoint.

Wilde:
Like two doomed ships that pass in a storm. We had crossed each other's way;
But we made no sign, we said no word, we had no word to say;
For we did not meet in the holy night, But in the shameful day.

Morrison:
Riders on the storm, Riders on the storm,
Into this house we're born, into this world we're thrown,
Like a dog without a bone, an actor out alone,
Riders on the storm.

Wilde:
I only knew what haunted thought quickened his step, and why,
He looked upon the garish day with such a wistful eye,
The man had killed the thing he loved, and so he had to die.

Morrison:
There's a killer on the road, His brain is squirming like a toad,
Take a long holiday; Let your children play,
If ya give this man a ride, Sweet memory will die,
Killer on the road...

Wilde:
Yet each man kills the thing he loves, By each let this be heard,
Some do it with a bitter look, Some with a flattering word,
The coward does it with a kiss, The brave man with a sword

Morrison:
Girl ya gotta love your man, Girl ya gotta love your man,
Take him by the hand, Make him understand,
the world on you depends, Our life will never end,
Gotta love your man.

Wilde:
Some love too little, some too long, Some sell, the others buy,
Some do the deed with many tears, And some without a sigh,
For each man kills the thing he loves,
Yet each man does not die.

Morrison:
Riders on the storm, Riders on the storm,
Into this house we're born, Into this house we're thrown,
Like a dog without a bone, An actor out alone,
Riders on the storm.

Wilde:
He did not pass in purple pomp, Nor ride a moon-white steed.
Three yards of cord and a sliding board, are all the gallows need,
So with the rope of shame the Herald came, To do the secret deed,
I walked with other souls in pain, within another ring,
And was wondering if this man had done,
A great or little thing, When a voice behind me whispered low,
That fellow's got to swing.

The cemetery audience hasn't waited for the final chord to fade away and rises in unison to acclaim the performance. Against a crescendo of applause and shouts of Bravo, bouquets that earlier in the day rested at the foot of neighbouring graves are being thrown at their feet. Colette and Piaf clutch white lilies and each other in sheer delight. Morrison and Wilde bow deeply with an affected humbleness. Their exchanged conspiratorial glances however betray the triumphalism coursing through their veins.

'They like, us Morrison, they like us.' Wilde exclaims as they rise from their sixth bow. 'At last we've done something right. I could kiss you. I might even find it in my heart to forgive you for the terrible castration you perpetrated on my effigy if you were to confess. Are you man enough, have you the balls? Declare your guilt to me and our audience. It will serve as our encore, and I shall then say no more. My balls can rest in pieces.'

'Wilde, if I had your balls I'd stuff them up your fu....'

Colette has stepped between them, drowning out the curse mid-obscenity. Bip and Piaf hold the men by the elbow, pointing them towards their vacated seats in the audience. The years have fallen off Colette's frail shoulders and she is once again the sassy burlesque artist with an audience in her hands. They fall silent as she lifts her arms, ready to address them.

'Finale time! Mesdames et Messieurs, I have a very special announcement to make. Rather a denouement, the explanation of a grave plot at this grave's plot!'

Bip mimes a groan and arches over, pointing to the tombstone carving and scratching his head.

'With the help of my good friends, Edith and Marcel, I shall lift the curtain on a mystery that has been played out for too long. Messieurs Wilde and Morrison, will you please take your seats?'

This time it is Wilde who groans. 'I fear, Morrison, that we are to witness grand larceny. Our thunder is about to be stolen.'

Colette cuts short his protest with a brutal strike of the keys for the opening notes of *Thank Heaven for Little Girls*. Bip is miming the words: clutching his heart, raising his

Ballad of Jim and Oscar

hands in thanks. His movements made all the more eerie by his shadow projecting on the pale limestone tomb as he moves between the candles. When the chord fades, it is the diminutive figure of Edith Piaf who steps forward and speaks the first verses of the song.

The audience is nonplussed and silent as the Little Sparrow's powerful vibrato fades away. Bip at first appears to imitate their uncertainty. His hands, which have been clasped under his chin, as if praying for an answer, start to lift in an arc. His expression is no longer sweet and sentimental but has taken on a much darker mask. He arms are now fully raised and his fingers interlocked. He is moving his elbows in and out in a cutting motion. The shadow projected on to the tomb draws a gasp of recognition from the audience. The silhouette of a giant pair of shears is hovering above the demon angel, snapping like a crocodile as it descends into its lap. Colette's playing of *Thank Heaven* is slow and deliberate, her voice strong, unrepentant.

Thank heaven... for my secateurs,
For secateurs made my Willy pay,
Thank heaven for secateurs,
They did the job in the most frightful way,
His beady eyes so helpless and appealing
One little slash sent him crashing through the ceiling,
Good heavens! thank heavens....'

She continues playing softly but leans forward to look at Wilde in the front row before speaking the next lines.

And then one day, what can I say?
Those balls turned to stone, found my graveyard home and haunted me ever after.
Thank heaven, mes amies, I had the answer.
For no matter where, no matter who, I knew just what I had to do.'

Her face lights up with joy, she pumps the accordion, fingers flashing across the keys beckoning Piaf to join her in a chorus duet:
Those great big balls in the moonlight,
They were gleaming,
With one swift blow, they lost their glow
And Oscar's jewels were sent a' reelin'
Good heaven, let's all thank heaven,
For little g...i..r...l...s...

While they hold the last note, Bip moves along the topiary hedge, snipping stalks and gathering a clutch of the shaped globes. He juggles four but allows two to drop heavily as he grabs his crutch in feigned agony. The two remaining ones are caught by Colette and Piaf and they finally allow the note to die. The audience explodes with applause, but even that cannot match the volume of Morrison's loud guffaws. Wilde by contrast is thunderstruck.

'This is an outrage' he starts to splutter, 'I call upon the authorities to...'

His protests are lost in a rousing cheer as two leafy globes hit him on the head. Colette picks up her accordion

Ballad of Jim and Oscar

while Piaf lifts her arms to the ecstatic audience to signal they must join in the encore they demand. Apart from a semi conscious Wilde there are only two others who don't take up the invitation. Behind the towering headstone Rich and Lizzie listen to the carousing until the final verse, only then softly singing the words to each other.

For no matter where, no matter who,
She knew just what to do.
A moonlit attack, an eerie crack
And Oscar's prizes were sent a' reelin'
Thank heaven, Good heaven,
Little Girls.

This time the last note has no time to linger. A lightning bolt and the mighty crack of thunder announces the imminent arrival of the storm. Before the rain can fall another flash of blue light warns of another arrival - les flics. Their squad car is outside the cemetery gate, blue emergency light strobing like an eighties disco. Bip reacts in the only way he knows how, racing round the tomb with his wrists crossed, as if handcuffed. The rain comes down like stair rods, dousing the candles and clearing the site of all traces of most living things (and all those not) the exceptions being a Canadian and an Englishwoman, who the cops find hiding behind a headstone.

The morning following midsummer's day and the sun is shining on the City of Light.

The waiters in the surrounding cafes of Gare du Nord

are indifferent. More concerned that the 10am Eurostar train to London has left and they can take a short break.

Lizzie Chace and Rich Hunter weren't aboard, but had been served breakfast: a cold croissant apiece and a tepid coffee in plastic cups, by the custody sergeant at the 19th arrondissement police station.

Far from being indifferent about the weather, he is furious that he must forfeit his day in the sunshine of his garden because he has to deal with two lunatics brought in on his shift last night.

'Your story is ludicrous. There was no Bip, no actors. The cemetery was empty but for you two hiding behind a gravestone,' he rails.

'The old metro line you describe closed many years ago and is sealed off. Your explanations have many flaws, including the fatal one. All the people who assisted you are dead. If there was spirits involved they were the sort found in a bottle. In short you have completely wasted my time.'

Rich is tired of trying to look contrite. 'Don't suppose Bip would have much to say for himself even if you could find him. And who's going to believe a guy who turns up in court wearing a pair of black tights?'

'Be quiet, you Americans talk too much. Despite my suspicions, the doctor says you are not drunk or drugged. Therefore we have decided that you must be mad.'

'Gee, thanks. That's the second time in two days I've been diagnosed,' Rich says with dripping sarcasm.

'But not crazy enough to be locked up at the expense

Ballad of Jim and Oscar

of the French taxpayer,' counters the cop.

'That'll be all the Brits down in the Loire, I guess,' Lizzie mutters beneath her breath.

'We can always change our mind, of course. You Rossbeefs have a saying, I believe, "Time to eat the Humble Pie," No doubt it is as hard to digest as the rest of your food. I suggest you take a large slice Mademoiselle Chace and give the rest to your American boyfriend.

'I'm not American...!'

'And you're not my boyfriend!'

'Yet,' says Rich confidently.

'Please, you may carry on your quarrel outside the station. But first you must sign for the belongings we took off you for your own safety. Wallet, purse, train tickets jewellery and this....'

He holds out a pastel blue box tied with ribbon, of the type popular for taking home fancy cakes from the patisserie. A message is written on its lid in neat script: *Il n'y a pas de rose sans épine.*

'It was handed in at the counter by an old lady who insisted it was given to a Mme Chace and Monsieur Hunter who were staying with us.' he says, nodding to the package, making it making it clear it was to be opened in front of him.

Rich grabs the box and tears the lid off with undue force.

'A Bottle of Jack Daniels' he shouts out, holding it aloft. 'With a big red lipstick kiss on it.'

Lizzie smiles, uncertainly. Puzzling over the message

on the box and one word that eludes her feeble French.

'Sans épine, without what?' she mutters to herself.

The sergeant is also puzzled, but by Rich's reaction. He was sure the Canadian had read and understood the message and had torn it because he didn't want her to see it.

'It is an old French saying, Mademoiselle,' the sergeant says, fixing Rich in his glare: 'There is no rose without a thorn.'

6.
The Boys are back in town

GALLOWS humour is being served with the ushers' morning cuppa at Birmingham Coroner's Court.

For Darren and Kevin, who are facing eight hours of empathising with misery, it comes as naturally as stirring in two sugars.

'See we've a got a bloke who fell under the tram at the Hawthorns station,' Darren says, scanning the day's list of inquests. 'He was taken to wards 6, 7 and 8 at the Queen Elizabeth Hospital.'

Kevin laughs even though they crack this one every time they have a rail death. He's soon rewarded for his loyalty. Darren returns an inch-perfect pass.

'Yeh, south Londoner, came up for the Palace match at West Brom. Terrible result for them, lost 5-2.'

Kevin volleys it into the net. 'Over-run and flattened, then.'

There is a single knock on the door of their office-cum-tea room, the signal that the Coroner is ready to begin. Time to face the first wave of grief.

Christine, widow of Derrick 'Dessy' James Glasser, the couple's eldest daughter, Crystal, aged 19, and a fresh-faced solicitor not much older, are escorted to the front row of cheerless plastic chairs. As with the unwritten etiquette of a funeral chapel, the row is reserved for the family, being the closest to the Coroner and the witness stand. Kevin gives Mrs Glasser a reassuring touch on the shoulder and smiles thinly as he guides her to her seat. She looks composed, but then it has been four weeks since her husband's death. She's convinced herself she's faced the worst. They all do, in Kevin's experience. He notices the Coroner's Officer slipping into court, shepherding the witnesses. No-one's even pretending to put on a brave face. Christine Glasser may not have yet heard the worst.

April 16, 9.10am: The Coroner, Dr Robert Hood, opens the inquest.

'Good morning, ladies and gentlemen, and may I begin by offering the court's condolences to Mrs Glasser and thank her for attending.

'Let me make it clear straightaway that I am here to determine the cause of death; that is to say, the events leading up to moment on Saturday, March 19, this year, when Derrick Glasser's life ended. It is not my role to apportion blame. It is for the police to decide whether there has been any criminal offence committed.'

Christine Glasser gasps in surprise, even though the Coroner's Officer had previously explained this possibility to her. The Coroner, anxious to avoid adding to her distress, pauses sympathetically for a moment but presses on without comment. He says the physical cause of death is beyond dispute. The pathologist's report is explicit: Mr Glasser died instantly from multiple injuries, commensurate with being run over by a tram. He did not say, nor did he need to, that Derrick Glasser's head had been severed. His widow had seen what remained of the body and it would haunt her for the rest of her life. However, he was duty bound to reveal that the report found that the 52-year-old had consumed the equivalent of three pints of beer that day and there was evidence of chronic heart and liver disease.

'To summarise, Mr Glasser was not the healthiest of middle-aged men, a factor that may have contributed to the fatal fall onto the tram lines,' he says.

'We shall hear differing accounts of the journey to and from the game, the mood of the fans, and in particular a description of the Crystal Palace fans' encounter with two teenage girls. Relatives of Mr Glasser, their legal representatives and others who are connected directly with this incident may ask questions of the witnesses here today.'

9.30am. Witness 1. Crystal Palace supporter Mike 'Roly' Royall, aged 52, gives evidence.

He tells that court that he and Dessy along with four other workmates from an electronics distribution warehouse in Streatham travel to all the team's away games. Had done for more than 20 years, suckers for punishment.

'We are all Thornton Heath lads, went to the same school, stayed in the area. Diehard Palace fans...' He stops. Why are all the faces staring at him like that? Diehard. Bugger. He mumbles an apology in the direction of Christine and Crystal. Chris isn't going to last the course, she's already teary-eyed. How is she going to react when all that garbage about the teenagers comes out? Crystal looks sound, though. His god-daughter, named after the club, despite Chris's misgivings. She's a bolshie madam now, embarrassed about her name, desperate to fit in at uni where every other girl is an Amy or Ellie. She told him they take the mickey out of her behind her back... "Crystal Glass-er." Nasty little sods. Football is off their radar, thank goodness. She and Chris don't deserve this. The Baggies' fan who's following him into the witness box would have a lot to answer for.

'We met at the Fox in Brixton on the match-day Saturday for an early one, then took the Tube to Euston,' he says hesitantly.

'Virgin intercity gets us to Brum around two o'clock,

no problem. There are loads of Palace fans on the train, we're singing, lots of banter, and it's a good atmosphere. The other passengers didn't mind. We're a family club, small and friendly. A bit boisterous maybe but we don't large it up like Chelsea and the Arsenal's glory hunters, sorry fans.'

'I'm sure all those passengers looking for a quiet journey to Birmingham were pleased with the entertainment,' the Coroner says dryly.

'When you disembarked at New Street did you go straight to Snow Hill station to catch the tram?'

Roly hesitates for a moment as if struggling to remember, but no-one is taken in. The 'lads' – him, Dessy and a dozen other Palace fans had stopped off at a city centre bar before walking the five minutes or so to Snow Hill. There had been no alcohol on the train and with all the singing and what have you they were as dry as a desert. It was cutting things a bit fine, he admitted, but as long as the trams were running smoothly they reckoned there wouldn't be a problem.

`But as we shall hear from transport police later there was a problem,' the Coroner says.

'Yeh, there was. The tram was waiting for us, and kept on waiting for at least 15 minutes after we got on. It was worse than the Tube at rush-hour. The doors were kept open and fans just kept on packing in. We all started getting a bit edgy in case we missed the kick-off but the station staff took no notice. We are big lads, y'know, used to the hustle and bustle of London. But even we had to breathe in and reach up for the overhead rail to keep steady.

'Me and Dessy and the others felt sorry for the regular passengers and tried to make space for them but it became impossible. Unfortunately some of the other blokes – I won't call them fans – thought it was a bit of a laugh and kept egging on Palace fans to cram into our carriage.'

'Just let me stop you there for a moment, Mr Royall,' says the Coroner. 'We shall shortly hear from another traveller in that carriage who will give a quite different account. What can you tell me about two teenage girls you met?'

'Well, for a start we didn't meet them; they were standing in the carriage when we got on, sharing a messy burger, drinking from water-bottles. Usual teenage stuff. They were caught in the middle. I suppose they were about 13 or 14; skinny girls surrounded by all these burly blokes. We tried to give them a bit of breathing room but it got so tight they couldn't lift their arms up to eat the burger. They were okay about it. Thought it was a bit of a laugh having all these men around, old enough to be their dads, wearing football shirts.

'Dessy chatted to them a bit, only because he thought they might be nervous. Just everyday stuff. Where they lived, if they'd been shopping, which footballers they fancied. Trying to take their minds off the crush.'

'Did he ask them about boyfriends or make any comment which might be construed as having a sexual undertone?' the Coroner asks.

'No, that's a bloody....a lie, Your Honour. We were

trying to protect those kids. They were flirting with us, if anything. Wanted to know all about the big city, where were the best places to go, if we lived near any pop stars...harmless chit-chat.'

'I'm sure you were able to give them a good account of the bright lights of Croydon,' the Coroner says sarcastically.

'And Mr Royall, this is not a criminal court and I am not a judge. I am in fact a doctor but quite happy to be addressed as Coroner or Sir.'

'Can I ask Mr Royall a question, please?' says a trembling voice from the front. Crystal has her hand raised, as if back at school. Her mother tugs at her daughter's sleeve in a vain attempt to stop her. Roly's bravado jaw, weakened by the undermining of the Coroner's remarks, drops noticeably. The Coroner smiles benignly and nods his assent.

'Did Mr Glasser, my father, ask the girls about their favourite clothes, the material and colours?'

The question hangs in the air, along with its implied accusation.

'Mr Royall..?' the Coroner prompts.

'Er, yes, I think so. I can't remember. If he did, it was only an innocent remark, a bit of a laugh.'

'Are you satisfied with that answer, Miss Glasser?' the Coroner asks, noticing that the mother is now desperately clutching her daughter's arm, hanging on to it like a lifeline.

Crystal stares at Roly Royall until he is forced to look at her before she says coldly. 'Yes. Fully.'

'I am not,' the Coroner says. 'I would like to know how the teenagers reacted. Mr Royall?'

'They, erm, didn't answer. A couple of passengers pushed through to the exit and they wriggled through to follow. That was the last I saw of them.

'Look, a lot is being made about these girls, but it was nothing at all. I wouldn't know them from Adam if they were sitting here. Just a couple of silly kids, that's all they were...'

The Coroner gives him a disapproving glance and asks him to continue.

'We eventually get moving and get to the Hawthorns as the game's kicking off. It's a massacre. We are three down by half-time, it's turning into one of the worst results of the season, the team is getting slaughtered.

'During the break, the six of us grab a beer at the visitors' bar under the stand. It's as bad as the game and bloody expensive too. The performance is so poor we talk about having a Brummie Balti after the match at a place we passed in the city centre.

'It's easy to get split up leaving a football ground so we said if one of us got separated we'd wait for him at the Hawthorns Station, about a 10-minute walk from the ground.'

'And what happened next?' asks the Coroner, glancing at his watch.

'It was terrible. Within a few minutes of the restart we had conceded again, we were being hammered.'

'Mr Royall,' the Coroner says sternly, 'I remind you that we are here to get the facts of a real-life tragedy in which a man lost his life in the most horrific way. You may concur with the maxim that football is more important than life or death. I certainly do not and neither does this court. Please continue without the match commentary.'

'Sorry your Honour, Sir. We left before the final whistle thinking we'd avoid another crush on the tram. Sorry Chris, you know what I mean.

'Dessy decides he needs a leak before we set off so he nips to the toilets under the stand and me and the others set off for the station thinking he'll catch up in a few minutes. But he must have lost his way a bit because we get to the platform and he doesn't turn up.

'We were at the end of the platform, the farthest away from the stairs, thinking we'd bag an empty carriage at the front.

'There must have been a hundred of more fans crowding the platform so I couldn't see much, but I could hear the tram sounding its horn. Then one of the lads, Jerry, I think, points up to the stairs and shouts, "There he is, the silly bastard! Oi, Dessy!"

'I just catch a glimpse of him rushing down the steps, then he's lost in the crowd. It's the last time I see him. There's a deafening screeching of steel wheels and screams, but worst of all a sickening thud. I don't recall anything else. The medics say I passed out.'

10am: Witness no.2 West Bromwich Albion season ticket holder Haydn Ashmore, aged 64, gives evidence.

I've been a Baggies' fan, man and boy, he tells the court. Adding, in a trademark Black Country putdown, 'Well, someone has to be.'

His accent still carries a trace of his Sandwell upbringing although he's lived thirty miles away in Coventry for most of his life. He travels to all home games, courtesy of his free bus and rail pass.

'Quicker than getting to Coventry's stadium on the edge of nowhere,' he says.

'Yes, I'm sure, Mr Ashmore,' the Coroner says, not unkindly, being used to nerves setting witnesses off at a tangent.

'Perhaps, though, we could concentrate on the journey you took starting at Snow Hill Station on March 19.'

The Coroner has misjudged the witness. Haydn Ashmore is not nervous. He is well practised in facing an audience, both in his long career teaching primary schoolchildren and in countless am-dram productions, a hobby he's pursued since university drama groups lured him on to the stage. His seemingly irrelevant quips were for his own benefit, his way of playing himself in, establishing his character. He had some hard things to say. And he wanted the family, Christine and Crystal, to know he wasn't some random troublemaker sticking the boot in. He would give an honest and credible account. They would not thank him for it. Perhaps they would not hate him.

'The tram was as Mr Royall described it, hugely overcrowded. Mainly with Palace supporters wearing red and blue shirts. We were packed like sardines but they kept encouraging more fans to cram in.

'I wanted to get off but I couldn't move. Me and a friend were jammed up against a window behind Mr Royall and the man I now know was Mr Glasser. Dessy, they called him. There must have been about twenty to thirty others jammed in the area between the automatic doors. Nearly all older men in Palace shirts. In the middle were the two girls, trapped in the crush. They looked like frightened rabbits.

'It started off with a bit of banter; the men asking them for a bite of their burger, quizzing them where they were going. But it wasn't innocent, the girls probably thought so at first but I could tell they were being pulled out of their depth.

'There was a bit of a competition going on, led mainly by Mr Glasser, to see who could chat them up. It sounds daft, men three, four times their age, easily old enough to be their fathers, acting like that.

'But in a way, they would only have got away with it with very young girls. This will sound odd but it was if they were in their teens again, young bucks showing off. But it was more than that. They were bullying them too.

'I remember one in particular, he was maybe thirty-five or so, and had a gold chain on outside his shirt, saying to them: 'We were going to get a cab to the ground, that's what you'd call a taxi.'

'It was pathetic really. He was trying to be the big I Am, as if he was talking to star-struck young fans. In other circumstances it would have been laughable.'

The snort of derision from Roly Royall, who'd taken a

seat in the second row, disagreed. The Coroner interrupted, 'Let me draw the conclusions, please, Mr Ashmore. What you describe sounds unpleasant but not extremely so. Are you saying that these men were threatening the girls?'

'Intimidating them, more like. They weren't being physically assaulted in the carriage, no. And without the safety in numbers, I doubt any individual would have pushed it further.

'It was more than unpleasant, though. The mob mentality was at work, each man was trying to score points and it became pretty smutty. Innuendo about eating a big burger, whether their boyfriends had a Big Mac, that sort of stuff.

'The girls had cottoned on by then and tried to keep quiet. You could see they wanted to get away. Then it became a bit sinister. Mr Glasser asked them if they liked his shirt, was it nice and silky? Would they like to feel it…? They went bright red. The mob, that's what they'd become, started cheering him on.

'It was one of those moments when you wish you were a karate black belt and could weigh in and flatten a few. But I didn't, like every other person in that carriage I did nothing. Pretended I hadn't heard.

'The reaction from his pals just encouraged him. He started asking them if they wore silk pyjamas, did they have older sisters who did.

'To be fair, half of the fans by then were telling him to cool it, but he became aggressive, telling them to mind their own effing business.'

He looked at Christine and Crystal apologetically, trying to convey he was sorry to have to say this but it was the truth. The older woman looked up for a second, enough to show the blind hatred in her watery eyes. Crystal remained impassive but met his gaze. With the slightest of movements, imperceptible to even the Coroner, she gave the merest hint of a nod.

'Please carry on, Mr Ashmore,' the Coroner says. 'It seems this incident, distasteful though it was, is irrelevant to the tragedy that was to follow. But I want to examine every possibility to see if there is a connection. Can you recall if the girls were still eating their burger while all this was going on?'

It was a question that perhaps only four of those present didn't think was extremely odd. The police officer was one. He was sitting in a side seat, taking notes. The Coroner and his officer, of course. Haydn Ashmore was the other but he wasn't going to let on that he knew its significance.

'No, not when it started to get really crowded," he replies, looking suitably puzzled. They were sharing it when I got on but as it got more and more packed there wasn't room to sneeze let alone eat. I think they must have dropped it on the floor when they escaped, just before the doors closed.'

'Did you see it when you left the carriage, Mr Ashmore?'

'I couldn't see anything below shoulder height by that time, no. When the tram stopped we almost fell out.'

'Thank you, Mr Ashmore,' the Coroner says. 'One last

question: on your return journey, after the match, did you see Mr Glasser or these two girls.'

'No, I did not, Sir.' His only lie.

Noon: The hearing adjourns for lunch. The Coroner asks all parties to be back promptly at 1pm.

'What's the missus done for you today then, Kev?' Darren asks, peering over the table at his colleague's neatly wrapped lunch.

'What century are you living in? My wife would no more make my sandwiches than she would iron my shirts. These are egg and cress – in Slims, if you really want to know – all my own work, so are the creases in this shirt.'

Kevin slips off his jacket and puts it over the back of one of the plastic chairs borrowed from the court. Darren doesn't respond; he doesn't have clue what a 'Slim' is and takes out a chocolate bar from his pocket and fills the kettle.

'What d'ya make of that in there, then,' he says, affecting an expression of comic exasperation.

'Poor sod gets chopped to bits under a tram and all they can talk about is whether he chatted up some young girls.

'Who gives a flying puck what he said. If a bloke can't have a bit of spin now and again, what's the world coming to?'

Kevin bites his tongue. He doesn't know whether he can be bothered with this. They get on well enough so long as they just skate over the top of anything more serious than football and office gossip. Darren, at 37, is five years younger than him, divorced, but an enthusiastic client of several internet dating services. He announces his weekend scores on the Monday before the traditional lament about the Villa's performance. Kevin realises he's between a rock and hard place. If he doesn't respond, he'll have to listen to Darren's bedroom boasts.

'Men of 22 let alone 52 should know better,' he says.

'My daughter Jess is 13. Just a kid. If I caught some lecherous old git asking her about her clothes, I'd flatten him. I wouldn't need a train to help me.'

Darren looks puzzled, suspects the older man is just winding him up so cranks it up a turn.

'Come on, what did he do? Teased a couple of 14-year-olds, flirted a bit, and maybe got a twitch out of asking about their clothes. They are gonna have to face a lot harder come-ons than that before long, eh?'

'No they don't. That's the point you bloody Neanderthal. They shouldn't have to face it. These are kids. But forget the age for a minute. What he did was intimidation, bullying, he was on a power kick, dominating those girls and enjoying the sexual thrill.'

Darren was speechless. Kev had never spoken to him like that before. He knew at that moment that the superficial friendship had ended.

The silence was palpable in the tea room, both men stared into their cups. Darren took the last bite of his Marathon bar, and the gulp seemed to bounce around the bare walls.

'What about the bloody Villa losing to a late pen?' Darren offers up lamely as an opening to peace talks.

1pm. The Coroner takes a sweeping look around the court to check all are present and opens the afternoon session.

He announces the third witness, who is being ushered in by a flushed-faced Darren, still smarting from his dressing down. Sergeant Nick Williams is an officer with the British Transport Police, but he doesn't look like a cop. He's wearing a green jean jacket over a white tee-shirt. His hair is styled like a footballer's; shaved severely at the sides with a spiked mop above. Inevitably he has a beard, pretty impressive too, given that he can't be more than twenty-five and fair-haired.

He explains that he is a plainclothes officer with special duties regarding football hooliganism. He is on duty after this hearing, hence the clothes and nods to Christine and Crystal, by way of an apology. He is about to give his evidence when their solicitor stands up to his full five feet seven and addresses the Coroner.

'Sir, if I may remind you, at the start of this hearing you indicated that we were not here as part of police investigation. My client has been through an unbelievably traumatic experience. She has lost her husband in horrific circumstances and this morning had to listen to unfounded allegations about his behaviour with young girls. Are we now going to...'

'What we are going to do,' the Coroner thunders, 'is not for you to question. I have said that we are here to find out the causes of Mr Glasser's death. There may or may not be a separate police enquiry. But for the moment we shall hear what light Sergeant Williams can shed on events at the Hawthorns Station. Mr Williams, please continue.'

'Thank you, Coroner. I was called in to keep a watch on the departing fans at the station. Look out for known trouble-makers. Palace has a good reputation for travelling fans but you never know what might kick off.

'There had been a delay in getting the trams to the ground and the overcrowding had caused a few skirmishes. There hadn't been any trouble at the ground. But the away team got thrashed so the fans could expect to be baited on the way back. We had uniformed coppers on standby in the vans if there was trouble at the flash points, but it's a balancing act in these situations. Go in mob-handed and you can provoke a confrontation.

'That's where I come in. I travel with the fans as if I'm one of them. If I see trouble I radio in immediately and back-up will be there within a minute.'

The Coroner looks up from his notes and gestures for him to stop. 'So, you were unaware of any earlier incidents concerning Mr Glasser and his friends. There had been no complaints about alleged harassment?'

'None at all. It was only later, that is after Mr Glasser's death, this came to light following an appeal for witnesses to come forward.'

'Thank you. Tell us where you were prior to the tragedy.'

'About a yard from the foot of the steps leading from the footbridge to the platform. That way I could see everyone filing in and pretend to be looking for mates, while keeping an eye out for trouble.

'As usual most of the fans were clustered around the nearest part of the platform, causing a bit of a blockage. It was fairly good-natured, though. Fans from the smaller clubs tend to be more philosophical in defeat, even to a relegation rival. They don't have the expectations of the big clubs' fans, who take it as a personal affront if they don't thrash the opposition.

'At 4.55, I heard the tram coming down the line, normally they are silent but the driver sounded his horn as a precaution, knowing there would be a lot of passengers milling round.

'Fans were still streaming down the stairs behind me and I could hear raised voices. Someone was pushing through, knocking fans out the way.

'I heard somebody shout "Oi, there's Dessy," just before a heavily set man in a Palace shirt ran on to the platform. He was shouting at people to get out the way and tried to swerve round the cluster blocking him, but then he swung out to the edge of the platform. That's the moment I thought he'd been hit by a small bird, because something flew into his face and, as he turned, he lost his footing and slipped headlong onto the rails.'

The loud sobs of Christine Glasser break his narrative. Crystal hugs her mother but stares blankly ahead. The Coroner says there will be a short adjournment. But is himself this time stopped in his tracks.

Boys are back in town

'Thank you but that won't be necessary. My mother will be fine. Please carry on.' Crystal's voice is clear and authoritative. Normally the Coroner would have brokered no challenge to his authority. On this occasion he decides a wiser voice has spoken.

'The tram was travelling at just a few miles an hour but the driver had barely a second to react,' the policeman continues.

'He slammed on the emergency brake but it was too late. Mr Glasser fell directly in his path and was crushed under the wheels of the engine and several carriages. There was no chance he could have survived. His torso, what remained of it, was hanging in his shirt from the tram's buffers. Sadly, it stopped at the point where his friends were standing.'

The Coroner asks him to move on to the subsequent examination of the site, omitting the details about the recovery of the body.

'I tried to protect the area where Mr Glasser slipped, but you will appreciate that in the panic that ensued many feet might have trodden on it. People were rushing around in panic, some had fainted, it was utter mayhem for a while.

'However, on the flagstone where he slipped there was a skidmark trace of what on forensic examination proved to be gherkin and tomato sauce. On the lip of the platform where the skidmark tailed off were the remains of a bread batch, sesame seeds and minced beef. Mr

Glasser had it seems slipped on a beef burger.'

The Coroner posed the question on everyone's lips, noting the policeman's reluctance to volunteer the information.

'Is it possible that is what you saw just before the fall? That it wasn't a bird that hit him, but a beef burger?'

'The only honest answer I can give is that it is possible, but I simply don't know. If it was it must have been thrown from the bridge. There is no evidence to support that. Despite widespread appeals no-one has come forward to say they saw anyone acting suspiciously on the bridge, and there were hundreds of fans around. The CCTV cameras were on but not covering all of the angles. They reveal nothing out of the ordinary.'

He hesitates, clearly concerned about what he will say next, the reason for his reluctance to answer the question.

'The only conclusive proof would have been if there had been any remains of a beef burger left on Mr Glasser's face. Unfortunately that wasn't possible given the extent of his head injuries.'

This time the Coroner has no option but to suspend the hearing as Christine Glasser slumps to the floor having fainted.

4.15: The inquest has resumed after an hour's break and the Coroner is summing up.

'Ladies and gentlemen, Mrs Glasser and Crystal, I have taken the unusual step of bringing this inquest to a close, without hearing any further from witnesses. I can see no benefit under the scope of this hearing for it to continue.

'I shall formally record a verdict of accidental death. Whether or not Mr Glasser was hit by a burger and then stepped on it, is not relevant. It may have been thrown, it may have been already on the platform. It could not, by any reasonable deduction, have been purposefully thrown or left there with the intention of knocking him into the path of a train.

'I said at the outset that it was for the police to investigate if any crime had been committed. Their enquiries will continue.

'It is not for this inquest to criticise Mr Glasser's behaviour on the outward journey. He has not been on trial. But If I may impart of word of advice to his friends, I would ask them to take a good look at themselves. You are men, no longer youths. Your bodies may not be up to chasing up and down the country, drinking pints and acting as if life depended on a football game. Your minds should be ruling your actions in other ways too. How many of you can put your hand on your heart and say you acted in a dignified way on that tram?

'I leave you with that thought.'

4.40 pm. Inside the tea-room. There's an awkward silence as Kevin and Darren watch the kettle boil.

'That's one for the record books,' Darren says, once more conceding to Kevin's silence. 'Death by burger.'

Kevin decides to accept the hand of peace. He's got to work with this man whether he likes it or not.

'Assisted by a chopped gherkin too. What a pickle.'

Outside the Court, Roly and four pals are looking pleased with themselves.

'Result! Let's go and have a drink, lads,' he says.

'Dessy would have wanted it. And we deserve it after listening to that load of balls.

'It was obvious from the start it had to be an accident. Trying to smear his name over a bit of banter with two kids was the real crime.

'What's it coming to when every time you chat up a bird you're accused of being a perv?'

The other men don't answer. They are looking over his shoulder at the two figures approaching. Christine and Crystal Glasser.

Crystal has her arm around her mum's waist, guiding her along. Christine has a large handkerchief to her mouth and is sniffling, her eyes are red and puffy. Roly turns and walks forward to greet them, arms open ready to embrace.

'Chris, Crystal, come 'ere, let me give you a hug. Me and the boys are going to have a jar before getting the train back. Come and join us. My treat. We'll toast Dessy.'

Christine lets out a strangled sob and plunges her face into the giant hanky. Crystal's look of sheer contempt scythes him at the knees and he sags.

'What? What did I say?' Roly splutters.

'Toast. It's dad's cremation tomorrow,' Crystal replies.

Haydn Ashmore catches the end of the exchange as he leaves the court. He also catches a challenge from Roly's shoulder, too late to swerve as the bigger man moves deliberately into his path.

It's the sort of trick Roly imagined his heroes did in the tunnel when they lined up against the opposition. Let 'em know you're there, my son.

Ashmore instinctively says sorry. He's from an era when that's what you did, whether it was your fault or not. Same as you were taught it was polite to offer your seat to a woman on a bus or train, not abuse them. He smiles at Crystal and mouths 'good luck'.

There's half an hour to kill before the train to Coventry is due in at New Street and Ashmore hasn't eaten. No problem, he knows there's a fast food outlet opposite the station where he can grab a bite. Be appropriate too. As he makes his way there, he re-runs the events he'd described to the Coroner. He stands by every word. Except for…

He had left The Hawthorns at the final whistle that Saturday evening. The floodlights had been switched on late in the second half because it was overcast. He emerged from the stadium to an early twilight. Street lights were on and so too were the headlights of the stream of cars heading down the Birmingham Road for the M6.

The gaudiest light though was from the yellow and red illuminated sign above the Big One, 'Britain's Best-loved Burger' takeaway. He had a ready meal ready to pop in the microwave when he got home but was drawn in like a moth to a flame. The Baggies had won for a start, worth a small celebration, but he had noticed something else.

There's a small queue inside. And, right at the front, there they are. He's certain it's them; the two girls from the tram a couple of hours before. They must have been to the match. He hears their order being relayed to the kitchen: 'Two Biggy Burgers, both lettuce, onion, tom sauce. No gherkin pickle.'

By the time their order arrives, he is at the front of the queue. He stares after them as they scurry giggling out the door in the direction of the station.

'Sir, sir, did you want to place an order?' The Big One assistant is looking at him in the kindly way she does when her grandad drifts off.

'Er, yes, sorry. I want a Biggie Burger. Lettuce onion, red sauce and gherkin pickle,' he says.

'And can you speed it up please, I've got a tram to catch and I wouldn't want to miss it.'

.

7.
You Better, You Bet!

'Not good. Eighty-nine. That's not good,' the doctor murmurs rather too mournfully, nodding his deep brow in agreement with himself.

He pulls off the small peg which fits like a pencil sharpener on my index finger and places it on his own.

'There, that's more like it! Ninety-six!' he announces, blithely unaware of his smugness.

He peers again at the digital readout and adds, unnecessarily, 'But eighty-nine is not good. Not good at all.'

Just in case I'd not got the message this was not good, he clips the gadget on to the middle finger of my 5-year-old grandson, Horatio, who registers ninety-nine. He's with me because I'd been volunteered to collect him from school on the one afternoon I'd managed to wangle an appointment with the GP.

'Ah, but he's young, you see,' says the doctor, who must've trained at the Hospital of the Blindingly Obvious, looking slightly put out that he's been bested by a few points.

Horatio beams and, convinced that it is in fact a pencil sharpener, grabs it back off the desk, sticks his little finger in and starts to twist it around.

It was time for a moderate injection of sarcasm.

'If that's my life expectancy, I'll take eighty-nine, doc.'

'It's your oxygen level and it's...'

'Not good, I know, you've told me. My guess is it's linked to the chest infection that's been causing me to cough and wheeze for the past two weeks. The infection for which your locum a week ago prescribed a five-day course of antibiotics, which has had no effect.'

'That's what worries me,' he replies. 'They should have shifted it if it's a bacterial infection. There may be some more worrying underlying cause. I'm referring you to the Medi-Swat Team at the hospital. The unit's open till 8 o'clock tonight.'

Now I was worried. The journey to Coombe Pines General Hospital was not for the faint-hearted. A high price would be exacted before the night was over.

Battling through kamikaze traffic to the furthest outpost of the city limit is enough to set the pulse revving like a boy racer's hot-hatch at amber light. Long before you arrive at the bewildering maze of buildings and car parks the Satnav has given up pleading to be let out at the nearest bus-stop and is sobbing in a corner of the windscreen.

The chest pain begins as you park, a piercing stab straight into the wallet. Dick Turpin would have blushed to demand the parking toll from ailing travellers.

But not the hospital trust, who neatly pass the buck, several million each year, in fact, to the private sector.

'Ah, well, you see, the money doesn't go into our coffers,' the excuse goes. 'Car parking fees are set by the company heading the Private Finance Initiative.'

PFI, otherwise known as the Profit From Illness, paid for the hospital. The city and health authority grabbed the wealthy hand of private investors willing to stump up. They in turn squeezed them by the balls to cough up huge interest repayments.

Coombe Pines was one of the earliest PFI deals, and reputedly the most expensive.

The care v. profit collision course may account for the hospital looking like a bipolar Lego fan's design for a combined uni campus, shopping mall and airport terminal. Only the mental health unit and the hospice are easily found. Appropriately, the former near the site entrance and the other at the exit.

The general hospital is tucked away at the back of the vast complex, identifiable by the blue and white striped canopies of the market stall selling fruit and veg in front of the symbolic rotating door.

A fortunate few hundred get to park nearby, while the remainder circle like vultures scanning for tell-tale reversing lights of a car pulling out then swoop to get their bonnet in first.

Sometimes the ritual has to be abandoned dramatically as the air ambulance landing circle is on the upper floor of the car park next to A&E.

Once inside the hospital atrium, priorities become

clearer. A cappuccino at CostaBuck, a browse through the jewellery shop or boutique and then a flick through the showbiz gossip mags at the WH Spar outlet....

'Can I be of help, sir?' An elderly man with a volunteer guide badge and a sympathetic smile that supposes my cat has just died has spotted my hesitation at the revolving door.

'Yes, I like to buy a fake gold chain to complement my impending tan, a Lee Childs' crime thriller for the sunbed and a family-size packet of grilled beef fiery crisps for the journey.'

'Sorry, sir, can you say that again?'

'Medi- Swat Team.'

'Ah, yes,' he sighs, relieved that I hadn't missed the mental health centre on the way in.

'Go right at the convenience store, past bereavement services and the RAC counter, it's the corridor opposite the Sexy Sari boutique'.

I don't get chance to hand over the doc's referral letter at the Medi-Swat counter. A hive of medics, alerted by my tentative footsteps on the laminate faux floorboards, stop buzzing and three pairs of hands shoot up vying for my white envelope.

'I'll take that, thank you, Mr Nelson,' says Nurse-in-Charge, stepping forward assertively,

'Your doctor phoned to say you'd be coming. Date of birth?'

'Er, 25th of the sixth, eighty nine. No, sorry, not eighty nine, erm sixty two.'

'Car registration number and time of entry? It'll be on your ticket.'

'Is this really necessary,' I grouch, rummaging in my pocket, but handing over the white ticket nevertheless.

The question goes unanswered as N-I-C dictates the information to an eager underling who's hovering at her elbow like a bookies' clerk at the racetrack.

'Expiry time four hours, 25 minutes, and 15 seconds,' she says, with an emphatic stab of her stubby pencil on the clipboard.

'Not my expiry, I hope,' I proffer, but it's met with a stony silence.

It's broken by the interjection of a 30-something doctor from behind a computer he's been hammering throughout the exchange.

'Right, let's get cracking, we know the targets. ECG, blood test, x-ray, registrar's briefing, assessment. Dispatch,' he says, before turning to me.

'Good evening Mr Nelson, or may I call you Horatio? I'm Dr Alistair, the registrar. Better alert the eye department Nelson's here, eh?' he chuckles, extending a firm confident hand in my direction.

I wondered how long that would be in coming. I couldn't collect a prescription without being offered an eye-patch ('aha, never heard that one before') or visited an optician who could resist saying how good my right eye was, considering.

Young grandson had a lot to look forward to. I was outed before new school friends at the calling of my first register.

'Horatio Trafalgar Nelson?'

Here, sir.'

A history teacher, Creswell Crossman, then began asking the obvious question, but I pre-empted him with an embarrassed high squeak: 'No relation.'

The smirk on his face as the class erupted in laughter taught me an early lesson in the fine arts of cunning and revenge.

I confided in Crossman that the tradition of naming the eldest son in our family after the great lord admiral started not only because of the shared surname. It began in 1843 when Nelson's column was unveiled in Trafalgar Square.

Among the throng to witness the event were my great great grandparents, Albert and Daisy, who was eight months pregnant.

At the moment of unveiling, with thousands of eyes pointed skywards to admire the heroic figure, a lone white pigeon swooped from the clear blue sky and with pinpoint accuracy landed a deposit straight in Daisy's right eye, temporarily blinding her.

In the ensuing panic her waters broke and she was carried to the nearby Hospital of Stricken Saints in the Strand where she gave premature birth to a son.

As Albert and Daisy cradled the wrinkled little infant, they agreed there could only be one name for their newborn baby: 'Pigeon'.

Thankfully, a tactful midwife persuaded my simple forebears that Horatio Trafalgar Nelson would be manlier.

And that's what I told the history teacher, knowing from the gleam in his eye that he couldn't wait to get to the staff room and have a few more laughs at my expense.

I left it for two weeks before letting slip to Mr Hogworthy, our maths teacher and rival for the deputy headship with Crossman, that I had said it as a joke, never expecting anyone to believe such a ludicrous story.

Crossman left at the end of the school year for an administrative position at an English language college in France. He didn't take with him the sports teachers' leaving present of an admiral's hat, made in cardboard by year 5's art class, bearing the message 'Bon Voyage'.

I'm wondering if I might have the opportunity to spin the same yarn here, when all conversation stops. A dull throbbing permeates the building.

'Chopper!' shouts Dr Alistair. 'You all know the drill. I want exact touch down time and take-off, colour of the first paramedic's jacket, and the time – to the second – it takes to get the stretcher into A&E. Now get to it!'

With that the staff split into twos, pencils and notepads gripped like small arms, and break off in four directions, the registrar whipping them along before disappearing through an unmarked door.

I'm entirely alone, with only the growing sound of rotating blades for company, as his abandoned computer flickers and a familiar Cockney voice growls from the screen:

'Gerrr on it, my son.'

A stubbly Ray Winstone's chin is jutting out at me, his

head floating against a backdrop of the hospital. A garish lightning bolt logo flashes 'BET-MED'. The right side of the screen shows league table of sorts and what appear to be odds.

> *250662 v CPT*
> *Away win after extra time 4/1*
> *Home dispatch before expiry time 50/1*
> *X Ray during first 60 minutes 10/1*
> *X-ray FC 10 minutes   500/1*
> *Blood test; more than 2 hours 1/2*
> *ECG: under 90 minutes: 6/1*
> *Penalty shoot out in event of drawn diagnosis 3/1.*

There's something familiar about the first number, and something even odder about actor hardman Ray Winstone. It's not him but an impersonator who's donned a fawn crombie and Cockney Geezer persona.

'Alwright, medics, looking for a bit of in play action are we?' Phony Ray growls.

'Ere, old up, the latest odds for our live matches are on your screen now. Better lay off the night nurse and get on the dog and bone to the BET-MED line now and grab a piece of the action.'

Ray's orbiting head cross-fades to a sunburst bearing the catch line 'Supporting your hospital? You Bet!' as the computer screen blacks out.

I'm still trying to make sense of the table when I hear 'Mr Nelson, date of birth 25,06,62?'

A pale youth with sleeve tattoos is pushing a wheelchair at me, his expression outwardly friendly, but there's a quizzical look in his eyes. I feel like an eavesdropper caught at the keyhole.

'That's me,' I respond, aware that he's heard the computer shut down and still nagged by the familiarity of that number.

'Time for your X-Ray, Mr Nelson.'

'Well, that's quick, but I can walk, thanks.'

'The wheelchair's compulsory, Mr Nelson,' he says with a confidence that belies his teenage years. 'I'm Andy, your porter for this evening. Please sit on the chair.'

I do as I'm told and the chair emits a single bleep as it takes my weight.

'Right, we are off,' Andy says with urgency, pressing a stopwatch hanging from his tunic's breast pocket.

He's counting to himself as we head for the swing doors, anticipating the precise moment the infra-red sensor will trigger them open, suddenly leans to his right, knee touching the floor like a superbike champion, and glides through the opening, scribing a perfect quarter circle.

We may have brushed the paintwork, but the manoeuvre has lined us up perfectly for the dangerous straight along the corridor. Between us and the stainless steel doors of the lift lies a minefield of pyjama patients tottering along hooked up to saline drip trolleys while chatting to their visitors who are clutching armfuls of shopping and meandering across lanes with their wide loads like continental truck drivers just off the Channel ferries.

But Andy is in the zone. His breathing has slowed, although he's at full stride, and his eyes are locked on the lift. Long hours of virtual reality training on computer games, he reveals later, have taken him for supermarket trolley show-off to cool headed Formula 1 hospital wheelchair ace.

We reach the lift within a nanosecond of the doors shutting, thanks to Andy's deft use of the left-hand brake and a shiny floor which sees our backend overtake our front, sending us spinning into the elevator at a near-perfect angle.

'Bloody hell, Andy, you cut that a bit fine.' A fellow porter is at the back of the lift trying to calm his bed-bound patient who has ripped off his oxygen mask in alarm and is struggling to breathe.

'Gerr on it, my son, under 10 FC,' Andy answers with a stage wink.

Our arrival around the final corner into the X-Ray dept is a model of technique and showmanship. Andy is short of breath. He's running on adrenaline or what Alex Ferguson once described as a 'controlled fury' of his truly outstanding players.

Stooped low over the handle grips of the wheelchair, his panting breath condenses on my left ear, forming tiny rivulets down my neck. At the reception desk, two middle-aged women are standing, arms held aloft, evoking the partisan Wimbledon war cry with yelps of 'Come on Andy.'

You Better, You Bet

The young porter, struggling to maintain momentum, shifts weight on to his left leg and pushes hard for the finish, simultaneously gripping the right brake till it shrieks. It's the signal for him to drop onto his backside, releasing the brake in one fluid movement, and send us into a wide arc sailing into X-Ray, finishing with a 180 degree flourish.

The cheers of the receptionists are still echoing around the empty waiting room when the radiologist pokes his head out the door bearing the warning 'Entry Strictly Forbidden when the light is on.'

'Brilliant, Andy! I make that unofficially 9.50. You've done it, son. A record.

'Now it's after the lord mayor's show, I'm afraid. Machine's on the blink and it's going to be a while before the techy gets down here.

'Why don't you take 250662 for a coffee at CostaBuck and come back in, say, half an hour.'

The light goes on. The 40 watt one above my brain cell that's been struggling over that number. It's my date of birth. I'm the one that pitted against CPT, Car Park Ticket.

'Andy,' I snap, 'it's time we had a little chat. Cappuccino and confession time, my son.'

We make our way to the coffee shop in silence at a stately pace, I can feel the glow from Andy's burning face radiating guilt and embarrassment in equal measure.

His resolve breaks as I take a first sip of froth topping,

sprinkled with chocolate in the shape of a stethoscope.

'It's not what you think, well it is, but we aren't what you think. They've got a bloody shock coming... greedy bastards. It's a win-win they said. We'd be the pioneers, then it would be rolled out nationally to PFI hospitals. All the profits back into patient care.'

I face him full on, unaware that my serious head is being undermined by a foamy moustache.

'So, you're telling me that what I saw on the monitor is genuine? The hospital is running an online betting service, giving odds on whether patients will be seen before their car park ticket expires? That staff can take a punt on whether I have a blood test done in under two hours... get odds of 50/1 on me getting out before my ticket gives out!"

Andy looks genuinely shocked: '50 to one, blimey, that's not a bad punt. I'd have some of that if I wasn't already committed to...'

'If you weren't already committed to exposing the whole shebang for what it is, Andy,' interjects Dr Alistair, who's crept up behind us with Nurse-in-Charge.

'A money-grabbing scheme to bleed more money out the system through a ludicrous gambling gimmick, dressed up as major source of new funding for patient care and an incentive for hitting waiting targets. Or as you have realised by now, Mr Nelson, sitting targets.

'Our unit was chosen, rather commanded, to pilot the dummy runs, and we've played along. More than that, we've suggested a few embellishments to ensure the PR gurus will be holding 'Don't Resuscitate' cards should they still be breathing after being hung by their own petard.'

'Andy's performance was your idea?' I suggest, thinking of the 500/1 odds on X-Ray FC under 10 minutes. 'FC as in football club?'

'Not quite,' says Dr Alistair, clearly pleased with himself. 'Final Corner, the one into X-Ray you just sped into on the chariot of fire. The PR suckers fell for it. An 'ironic and playful reference to popular betting culture associated with football,' was how they described it.

'All the staff involved have been given a nominal fiver to bet this evening as part of the pilot. Guess where all the smart money's going?'

Nurse-in-Charge scribbles a quick calculation on her clipboard and beams. 'Roughly 200 fivers at 500 to one equals £500,000. All going, nominally of course, from the hospital coffers to the pockets of staff over a harebrained scheme.'

'Which is what we shall be revealing to the nation's Press tomorrow, Mr Nelson,' says Dr Alistair. 'And we want you to be there with us as the star witness to this ridiculous folly.'

I'm momentarily speechless. Not helped by Nurse-in-Charge miming a wiping movement across her lips, which though oddly attractive in the circumstances, I realise indicates I have a cappuccino moustache.

'Ah and how coincidental that I should turn up on cue as a guinea-pig the day before you tell all to the Press,' I manage to splutter, disconcerted by Nurse-in-Charge's lingering smile.

'Not a coincidence,' she responds. 'But very fortuitous nevertheless. Your doctor has been helping us by sending patients he thinks might be sympathetic to our aims.

'Your name stood out immediately. We brought forward our plans to meet the Press when you walked through the door. It was a chance too good to miss.'

My expression gives away my disappointment at the stupid name dogging me once again and I say nothing.

'Perhaps, I should explain that I too will be talking to the Press, Horatio,' says Nurse. 'I will be introduced as Emma Hamilton, a cross I have also had to bear during my career.

'I have lost count of the patients who've muttered 'Kismet' when I've told them I'm their nurse. Now I can use it to make sure a huge folly gets mega coverage.

'What editor could resist Nelson and Hamilton blowing the PFI gambling boat out the water. It's fate. It's kismet. Horatio, this is our Trafalgar.'

It was probably 'kiss me,' that Nelson whispered with his dying breath to his shipmate. And far more likely that's what Emma's patients whispered to her. But I can forgive her bending the truth.

'I'll do it,' I say leaving a pause for a but, as three anxious faces hold their breath.

'My expiry time was 4 hours 25 minutes and 15 seconds. Andy's got Four minutes 10 seconds to get me to the car park.

'Geer on it, my son, I've got an early start in the morning.'

8.
Oh, No! Not Romeo

BUSTED, disgusted, agent can't be trusted.

That just about summed it up as Ben slowly got a foothold on reality after a tormented sleep. This can't go on indefinitely. Wasn't that how the song went? They were right. It got worse.

'Over a million hits. You've gone spiral, Benjamin. You're famous.' His flatmate's gratingly-posh voice shatters any lingering hopes he had that it was all a bad dream.

'Viral, you stupid tosser, and I don't wanna be famous, Jez. Not on YouTube anyhow.'

Ben crawls out of bed, still in his jeans and tee-shirt looking like he's spent the night on the London pavement. Jeremy is in what he calls the sitting room, staring at his laptop, nearly wetting himself although he must have watched the clip a dozen times already.

'Oh god...' Ben groans, poking his head round the door and seeing himself on screen. As stitch-ups go this is the work of a master craftsman. The video begins a little shakily, slightly out of focus. Just enough to have you believe it was a chance iphone job. But no opportunist amateur would have taken the trouble to add captions like the one at the bottom of the picture:

12.30pm. July 10, 2016. London. Tour guide Ben Wyman with party of Japanese tourists.

And there he is, in full tour guide pomp outside a narrow terrace house on Bankside, just yards from a choppy Thames, pointing up at its wrought-iron balcony. Bullshitting for Britain.

'This, ladies and gentlemen,' Ben announces with a theatrical wave, 'is where the young and ambitious William Shakespeare lived when he arrived in the capital from Stratford.

'The original house where he rented a room was destroyed in the Great Fire of London. When it was replaced the owner insisted it should have a small balcony exactly the same as the one in Shakespeare's day.

'Why should that have been so important?' he asks.

The camera artfully picks out puzzled faces. Some clearly haven't a clue what he is on about. A few are mouthing the titles of the Bard's plays. With the guile of a phony spiritualist, Ben plucks a winner out the air. 'Yes, Madam, you at the back. Did you say Romeo and Juliet? Exactly right.

'For this is where many believe England's, nay the world's greatest playwright, conceived the idea for the star-crossed lovers' famous balcony scene. It was the work of a genius to transpose a humble balcony in what was then in a squalid part of East London to Italy's Verona, a cauldron of passion and violence.'

Jeremy probably was wetting himself at this moment.

Ben wouldn't know as he's got his hands clasped over his eyes and is kneeling face down on the floor.

Oh No! Not Romeo

He peeks between his fingers unable to resist watching his humiliation again, praying that it can't be as bad as he remembered. If anything it's worse. He's framed perfectly, looking imploringly at the balcony. The camera has started a slow zoom in as he speaks.

'This, ladies and gentlemen, is thought to be the very spot that inspired that famous lovelorn plea: "O Romeo, Romeo! Wherefore art thou, Romeo?"'

The balcony doors burst open and the answer comes in a bellowing bass profundo: "Oh, Oh, that Romeo, He's gawn away, left me on my own-ee-o, I'm so alone-ee-o."

None of the startled Japanese spectators would have been expected to put the name Florrie Forde to the rotund figure looming above them. If by remote chance any had recognised the parody of the music hall star's famous lament for the loss of Antonio and his ice-cream cart they would not have pictured her as bulbous-nosed and bearded, wearing a green curly wig and frilly frock.

Ben, however, knew instantly who it was and where the costume came from. Dave Jennings, wearing Mr Toad's washerwoman disguise for the jail escape scene in St Paul's College of Music and Drama's Christmas production of Toad of Toad Hall.

Jennings is giving it his all, milking the polite applause from the baffled Japanese with elaborate bows, rising to wipe an imaginary tear from his eye, blowing diva kisses in response to the cheers coming from the deck of a passing river tour boat.

'No please, please, you mustn't... you mustn't stop

applauding,' he shouts.

'Jennings. The utter bastard,' Ben whimpers into the carpet. The video continues mercilessly, capturing him open-mouthed, unable to speak. He couldn't look more foolish if his pants had dropped down.

Jennings is scattering rose petals from a wicker basket which fall like confetti on the Japanese tourists. The final frame freezes on a close-up of Ben as one hits his nose. Across the bottom of the picture, words are appearing as if it were breaking news:

Tragedy...Ben Wyman...Shakespeare's London Tours.... Alas.

The video fades to black and Ben collapses full length onto the grubby carpet, providing a further hurdle for a cross-legged Jeremy who's struggling to get to the toilet. From the back pocket of Ben's crumpled jeans the theme tune to Thunderbirds breaks out from his mobile. Reality calling.

He looks at his watch. It's not yet 8am, none of his aspiring actor mates would be awake for another four hours. It'll be Sam from the office. He guessed she'd be handed the job of telling him he was sacked. The boss of the walking tours company, Charlie Emerson, knew he fancied her. It wouldn't be enough to simply fire him. This would be his way of twisting the knife before disposing of the body.

Fat chance of Charlie shouldering any blame, Ben thought. He'd warned him that the City trader who owned the Bankside house was pissed off at seeing groups of tourists gawping at his pied-à-terre while being told a cock and bull story. If Charlie had listened and restricted that part of the tour to weekends there wouldn't have been a problem. The owner was at home in the Cotswolds playing the devoted husband and father to wife and children.

But not before spending Friday afternoon with a girlfriend at his Bankside love-nest. His 'one for the road' performance as he liked to call it. But last week he lost power on the home straight when his mistress burst out laughing at Ben's commentary going on outside the window. The furious trader rushed out in just his silk boxers looking as if he intended to bulldoze Ben into the Thames but slammed the brakes on his temper a centimetre short of his ear.

'This house never even had a bloody balcony until the late 1960s,' he bellowed into it, adding a few choice words for the foreign tourists which needed no translation.

Ben was deaf in that ear for two days. Charlie was however deaf in both ears to Ben's pleas that they should ditch the balcony from the Shakespeare tour itinerary. He regarded the story as one of his best innovations. Just be a bit quieter on Fridays, eh, Ben, wink, wink.

And this was the result. Total humiliation. Ben had become a laughing stock.

The City dealer probably earned more in bonuses than the Chelsea football team. A fistful of fivers would be loose change to him but a small fortune to Dave Jennings, who he'd doubtless bribed. But how had they got together? It was too much of a coincidence that his nemesis from drama college should be the star turn in the stunt. The likeliest scenario was that Jennings, who shared the same agent as Ben, had got wind of the run-in with the love-rat trader and nipped along to offer his services. Slimy sod.

The Thunderbirds theme was still ringing. Time to face the music.

'Ben, you had better get into the office quick, Charlie is going demented.' Sam's usual husky voice had risen a notch in pitch.

He considered playing the innocent, if only to coax a bit of sympathy from Sam; decided instead he'd play the heroic card and fell on his sword.

'Tell him I'll bring in my badge tomorrow,' Ben said, as though he was quitting the NYPD. 'Have my P45 ready and I'm gone.'

Sam wasn't in the mood to play along. 'Ben, I've been answering the bloody phone since Charlie dragged me in at seven o'clock. The world and his wife want to book on the Shakespeare tour and Charlie is running round like a dog with two cocks. So bloody well get your stupid arse in gear and get down here.'

Ben's 20-minute Tube journey from West Ham to Tower Hill was normally spent in monastery silence. Strict observance expected. And no eye-contact permitted with anything other than book or free newspaper.

At Stepney Green the order is breached by a couple in their twenties who've been huddled in a whisper.

'It's you, ain't it?' the woman rasps accusingly at someone whom Ben presumes is standing behind him.

'The Shakespeare guide,' her partner chips in, staring directly at Ben. "Oh! Oh! Romeo, I'm not at home-e-o," or summat. Bloody brilliant, you looked a right prat.'

The carriage doors open at Whitechapel, saving Ben from further punishment. He is out and up the stairs by the time silent order descends again as the train pulls away. He walks the remainder of the route with his hoodie pulled down and slips into the office like a thief.

Ben had hoped to have a few moments with Sam to get the lie of the land. If she hadn't cooled down by now, so much the better. Her vulgar Cockney was a treat after four years of listening to middle-class drama student Mockney. Sexy too.

He got as far as 'Hi, Sam' before Charlie burst in grinning like a Cheshire cat, brazen as ever in chalk-stripe suit and loud tie.

'Ben yooou beauty,' he gushes, rushing over to embrace his employee in a bear-hug. 'You're a diamond, my son, a genius, put us streets ahead of the snooty Blue Badge crew.'

He manhandles Ben into his office and onto the overstuffed green leather armchair reserved for clients. In the stream of Cockney consciousness that follows, Charlie's praise flows more fulsome than the Thames at ebb tide.

Not once does he allow Ben a word in edgeways or any other way. He claims to have had hundreds of calls from people desperate to go on the walk; radio stations hoping for a five-minute phone interview for the breakfast shows and their counterparts on TV willing to pay if Ben will appear on the sofa in doublet and hose. Two of the posh papers' star feature writers were waiting on a callback to see when they can interview him.

'The great British public think it's a hoot, Ben. They aren't sure if you were acting or not, but they love it. These are punters brought up on TV bloopers as entertainment; now spending their time surfing the Net for celebrities falling over, kangaroos skateboarding, or wardrobe malfunctions involving that family with the huge arses.

'And you've got them on a string, son. Even had me going. Your mate doing the music hall thing was a stroke of genius. Two in one, Shakespeare down at the Old Bull and Bush. Brilliant.'

Ben was pinned to the chair by the blitzkrieg, reduced to mumbling 'but it wasn't like tha…' Charlie sat back, serious-faced, and steadied himself for a momentous announcement.

'We've got to cash in, Ben.'

Charlie let the offer hang in the air, confident. But the silence lasts a beat too many.

There's a single rap on the door, immediately followed by Sam backing in, holding a tray of coffees, shortbread biscuits and a bottle of malt whisky. Ben is not so distracted by the sight of the secretary's backside, shapely though it is, to be blind to the fact that Charlie is choreographing the show.

'Listen Charlie, I'm flattered you think I was acting, but I wasn't. I was set up. And I was made to look a right idiot. It may be good business to you, but for me it's professional suicide. No disrespect to your firm, Charlie, but I haven't spent the last four years training to be an actor to end up being a stooge for a Carry On Up Shakespeare.

'The best I can hope for is it'll one day be forgotten and I can crack on with trying to get my first serious role. So thanks, but no thanks, I'll take my cards and be gone.'

Charlie didn't blink. He'd heard far worse insults. To his embittered rivals he was known as the pigeon. "Flies in like vermin, shits on everyone then leaves others to clean up the mess," was the politest interpretation.

Legend had it that he got into the business by chance, waylaid by a group of flustered Texans gathered outside Tower Hill Tube station. He was carrying a colourful umbrella and one of them assumed he was the tour guide they'd been waiting for. While Charlie was trying to explain himself, another of the party thrust a tenner into his hand saying, 'Charles Dickens' London Tour? Let's go, Buddy. No more fiddling about, eh! Baker Street here we come.'

Charlie led them away like a Pied Piper of East Ham. He just got them around the corner seconds before the real guide arrived, and didn't stop until Millennium Bridge. According to the story, probably started by Charlie himself, he told the Texans that this was the bridge, since smartened up a bit, of course, where Sherlock Holmes and Dickens fought over custody of Oliver Twist as a flood tide swept up the Thames. A drama later to be immortalised in print as the scene of Bill Sykes' death at The Reichenbach Falls.

After getting away with that and £200 in tax-free tenners, Charlie realised he'd found his vocation. Just needed to do a bit of work on his literary history.

'Thought you might say that, son,' Charlie says, looking at Ben with his kindly-uncle face on and handing him a biscuit.

'I was trying to hand you a face-saver, pretending that you were just playing along with the joke. But I knew you'd been framed, as Jeremy Beadle used to say, God bless him.

'I was on the blower to your agent this morning, got the full Monty from him, told me all about your feud with Dave Jennings, too.

'Let's be honest, Ben, if you quit now your chances of making it as a serious actor are zero. You are typecast as the stooge of a YouTube prank. It's out there in cyberland, or whatever they call it, and you can do bugger all to kill it off. But you can change what people think of your performance. Turn it on its head, come out with acting cred enhanced.'

Charlie dipped a Rob Roy shortbread biscuit in his coffee and stirred in a sweetener.

'Half the people out there think you were had, Ben. The rest aren't sure. One thing can convince them that you were not only in on the joke, but also a brilliant comic actor in the great Shakespearian tradition. Ben, we can give 'em The Bard meets Music Hall Part ll.'

Oh No! Not Romeo

Ben's coffee comes back up his throat for an unwanted encore, triggering a coughing fit. Charlie pours him a small measure of whisky. Sam tries to ease his embarrassment by pretending a sudden fascination with her text messages.

Charlie is unrelenting, 'You also get the last laugh on Jennings too, Ben. Think how he's going to feel when you get all the praise and he's cast as the clown.

'Once the new video is on the Net, we'll be able to set the agenda with the arty journos from the posh Sundays and magazines, same with the TV and radio. They'll be falling over themselves to hear your views on how Shakespeare would have embraced the Internet, had his own blog, Twittered his sonnets, etcetera. They'll be able to recycle all that guff about continuing the fine English tradition of bawdy humour, farcical misunderstanding, blah blah.

'Mark my words, Ben, by the time Christmas comes you'll be treading the boards in Stratford, upstaging that Dr Who bloke who's got his feet under the table at the Royal Shakespeare gaff.'

Ben has downed his malt and is pouring himself another. Sam is amazed, she thought he'd be halfway home by now or else passed out on the floor. But Ben could see past the hyperbole. The nub of what Charlie said was true. His career as an actor was dead in the water at the moment. If he didn't find another lifeline, a long career in bar work awaited him. Well, so be it.

'You've forgotten one thing, Charlie. It would need the same cast and there are two good reasons why Dave

Jennings wouldn't do it again. One, he hates my guts, and two, I'd bloody kill him if I ever saw the bastard again.'

He doesn't need to shout to emphasize his anger, his whisky glass does that when it shatters on the floor as he strides toward the door.

The fridge at Ben and Jeremy's two-bed flat is empty by 6pm. A half dozen bottles of beer and a bottle of cheap wine gone in one sitting. Jeremy has gone too. Left in protest at finding Ben incoherent, flat on his back, surrounded by the remains of his smashed laptop.

Jeremy is from a patrician family who believed in the idea of public service. While most of his public school friends spent their year out "travelling" on daddy's credit card, he was a volunteer in a Salvation Army hostel in Leeds. He emerged with a practical compassion: sympathy for the alcoholics and a close relationship with the mop and bucket. He left Ben propped up, his airways clear and a cold towel across his forehead. The remnants of his laptop could stay in situ. He'd give Ben a couple of days before he'd demand money for a replacement. Learned that too in Leeds. Soft touches get squashed.

Two hours after Jeremy had silently shut the door of the flat and most likely their friendship, Ben was still immobile but his mind had landed somewhere close to his head. He'd been reassembling the fragments of Charlie's plan. One big ugly shard called Dave Jennings just wouldn't fit. It didn't when they first met at drama school four years ago, when he was just an irritating splinter, now he was a fully developed sharpened shaft in the buttock. The feud was largely Ben's fault. He accepted that and during the first year at college tried to make amends for making the stupid joke. He was trying to impress, make his mark as the class wit, disguise his inferiority complex. Ben's family was solid working class, Labour-supporting. Salt of the earth, if you wanted to be patronising. And this middle-class lot certainly would, given the chance. Ironically, Jennings was the only other student in that year's intake who came close to working-class.

His roots were in Dorset farming stock; his broad shoulders a legacy of hard graft in the fields during the school holidays when he and his elder brother helped out. Jennings was sensitive about his background too and lacked confidence. He knew his acting abilities were limited and his looks were never going to make him a star. But he had a voice. A rich bass with a sweet tone, only given rein in the Dorset fields until a school music teacher heard the raw potential. He was soon spending more time in school musicals than at the farm. The voice had landed him a scholarship to study musical theatre at St Paul's.

It was at a get-to-know-you "Freshers' Mingle" that the most attractive girl in class asked him to name his favourite musical. No girl that stunning had ever asked him anything, other than to get out the way, and he was flustered. Ben, who like the others already had him down as a yokel because of his accent, saw his opportunity and jumped in: 'Is it Oklahoma?'

Jennings bristled and snapped back, 'Why should it be?'

'No reason, just thought you'd be a natural for the star role... y'know, leading tractor.'

It got the laughs but at a high price. Jennings was thereafter known by students as Tractor, even the staff started using it. Ben hadn't intended to be cruel, but the damage was done. At every opportunity Jennings would try to get revenge. His retaliatory jokes about Ben invariably fell flat. At parties they had to be separated so often one eventually had to be left off the invitation list. It was nearly always Jennings. Every time someone called him Tractor he hated Ben a bit more.

Ben tried many times to explain it was a spur of the moment gag. But after a few months he began to realise that Jennings was feeding off the hatred. All the taunts he had endured at school, the ribbings by his parents, the snide remarks at the Young Farmers' socials had been conveniently distilled into a poison called Ben Wyman. So he gave up feeling sorry. He loathed the self-pitying... what? Okay, bloody farm boy.

A single rap on the front door interrupted his deliberations. None of his mates would give one tap. It was more a business rap. The thought propelled him out the bed oblivious to the scraps of laptop strewn across the floor.

'Sam... what, what are you doing here? I mean, sorry, come in, the place is a bit of a...'

'Shithole would cover it.' Sam is standing in the doorway, holding a carrier bag, looking with disdain at the carpet.

'And you don't look much better, Ben. You look as though you've been...' she stops, staring at the towel around his neck and the vomit stains on his shirt. 'I've bought a takeaway curry and, well, something to drink. Perhaps another time, though, eh, Ben?'

He's glazed over. Was this still the drunken haze? Sam the office fantasy, a tantalising dream. Out of his league. But here she is, the sexiest women in London. And here he is, caked in vomit, wet towel on his neck, head thumping.

'No, don't go, Sam. I'd love a curry,' he lied. 'Need to clean up a bit, though. Why don't you pour yourself a glass of wine and put the food in the kitchen while I have shower?'

'Blimey, you don't hang around do you? Girl knocks on your door and you're ready to get your kit off before the wine's uncorked,' she says, arching her eyebrows in mock surprise.

It's not until Ben is under the shower that he realises he hasn't taken in any fresh clothes to change into. Getting to his bedroom would mean a dash across in full view of Sam, with only a hand-towel for cover. He poses in the mirror to see what's in and what's out, and spots Jeremy's dressing gown in the reflection, hooked on the door. Any normal bloke of Jeremy's age would have a bath robe, if anything at all. A dressing gown, maybe, if he was being ironic and got it cheap in the charity shop. Jeremy bought his new, to mark the 40th anniversary of the death of his favourite playwright, Noel Coward, copying The Master's penchant for flowery gowns with satin cuffs.

Sam had kicked off her heels and was trying to make herself comfortable on the lumpy settee when Ben emerged looking like an eccentric great aunt in an Agatha Christie play.

'You can't be serious,' Sam says, straight-faced. 'You haven't sipped champers from my slipper yet or told me Samantha was your mother's name. What happened to the seduction build up?'

Ben, pink as a boiled lobster, mumbles something about getting dressed, be out in a minute, and shuffles into his bedroom. When he returns he's dressed in fresh tee-shirt and jeans. Sam is humming a jaunty old song while dishing the curry out onto the only two plates she could find amid the abundance of glasses.

'No dinner jacket and cummerbund tonight, then, Mr Smoothie,' she teases.

Ben, having recovered most of his senses hijacked by alcohol, pretended to be embarrassed but was enjoying the flirting and embellishing the events following his dramatic exit from the office. Truth was he enjoyed being the object of Sam's attention, even if he was being sent up. She was maybe only two or three years older than him but if she wanted to play Mrs Robinson he was up for graduation.

'You haven't asked me why I'm here yet,' she says, not waiting for an answer. 'I was worried about you, the way you reacted to Charlie. When you didn't come back

I phoned your mobile and your flatmate Jeremy answered. He was very diplomatic but told me he'd come home and found you Brahms and Liszt, flat out, surrounded by bits of his smashed laptop.'

She lowered her eyes, a faint blush appeared in her cheeks which she tried to disguise by clumsily gulping the last of her wine. She got up and moved to the settee, patting the seat next to her and looking straight into Ben's eyes. A faithful whippet couldn't have moved quicker. But as he turned to face her, Sam's eyes dipped again

'Look, Ben, it's really none of my business, and I admire your stand against Charlie, but I think he was right. And I think you know it too. Charlie would fire me if he knew that I was here but I can tell you he's spent the whole day trying to come up with another idea to help you.

'I'm not saying he's not also trying to help himself. He wouldn't be Charlie if he wasn't. But if that means you get your career back on track, so what? I want to see you on the telly or in the West End, so that I can boast about you to my girlfriends when you finally get round to asking me out.'

She turns away coyly, brushing Ben's leg as she reaches down for her shoes. He moves towards her but Sam is up on her feet looking, for once, slightly unsure of herself.

'Now, in case I fall for the charms of a toyboy with a sexy dressing gown, I'm going. A taxi's picking me up outside in two minutes. Sleep well, Ben, but think on about my advice.'

He didn't. Sleep well, that is. Too many things on his mind. Mainly concerning Sam and X-rated. It wouldn't be wrong to say his heart was ruling his head when he phoned Charlie, but not wholly true. Another part of his anatomy was pointing the way too. As for Jennings, Ben would only agree to do it if he didn't have to speak to him.

By 11 o'clock Ben was climbing the stairs to the office again. If there was any humble pie to be eaten, Charlie deserved the lion's share.

Sam legs appeared. At least that's all he could focus on from mid-stairway as she came out of her office. When he looked up he saw she was holding a finger across her lips. The message was clear: not a word to Charlie about last night. Then she blew a kiss. At that point career-minded Ben abandoned ship and infatuated Ben took the wheel with both hands. No compass needed.

Charlie greeted him as if yesterday hadn't happened. Take a seat Benno, my son, pour yourself a coffee, good of you to come in. I've given a lot of thought to how we can work together on this project to achieve a favourable outcome. Charlie had been listening to Radio Four again. He had a habit of picking up MP-speak from the morning guests under pressure. It was the sort of phrase that could apply to any situation. Ben had heard it before, fully expected Charlie to soon be calling him a stakeholder in the firm's future.

'Take a look at this, Ben,' Charlie says, taking two sheets of typed A4 off his desk and handing one to him.

'It's gotta be the perfect vehicle for your next video. Wrote it myself after a bit of research.'

He points to a copy of A-Level Study Notes for Shakespeare's Plays and Sonnets, and sits back smugly while Ben scans the sheet.

It takes him five seconds.

The Boy I love is out in the Galleon/William Shakespeare's play Antony and Cleopatra.
Cast: Ben Wyman as the tour guide and Dave Jennings as Cleopatra/Marie Lloyd.

'I know, brilliant isn't it?' Charlie says, pretending to mistake Ben's lost-for-words bewilderment as stunned admiration. 'One little change, gallery to galleon and it all falls into place.

'Course, I don't expect you'd know the song, but you still hear it in some of the old boozers in the East End that have a sing-along on Saturdays. Marie Lloyd made it famous, one of the all-time greats, bit before your time. Mine too. More my dear old grandma's era. You might recognise the tune…'

Charlie puffs out his chest, stares at the ceiling striplight and starts to sing in an exaggerated Cockney.

The Boy I love is out in the galleon,
The boy I love is looking now at me…

Proud as a Pearly King, he pauses for praise and is met by silence, so continues.

There he is, can't you see? Waving his handkerchief,
As merry as a robin that sings on a tree.

'I don't know what to say, Charlie, I've heard that tune somewhere recently. It's not a million miles from Oh, Oh Antonio but then all those old music hall songs sounded alike. For the life of me I can't see how you can work that one with Antony and Cleopatra.'

'That's because you haven't had a butcher's yet of my treatment,' Charlie replies, looking as if he'd improved on the Bard's original.

'I've kept it loose, don't want to make it look as if you've been scripted, given you a bit of improv room.'

He hands the second sheet over, affecting a modesty which Ben immediately sees is well deserved. This is barely an outline.

Setting: 2pm Wednesday, The Golden Hind Tudor warship at Pickford's Wharf, Clink Street (a few minutes' walk from Shakespeare's Globe Theatre).

Dave Jennings will be in situ, out of sight on deck behind the mast, dressed in his music hall drag gear, ready to pop up on cue and belt out his song. He'll be right above Ben and his group on the quayside.

Ben's group of Chinese tourists (waiters I know from the restaurants up West, who'll be dressed for the part) will be told to gather in a circle in front of him facing the boat.

Ben's lines: Shakespeare trod this very street, built the Globe theatre up the way, and lived around the corner. On this actual wharf, now fittingly the berth of a Tudor warship, he sought inspiration between shows. Perhaps puffing on a pipeful of tobacco brought home on this very ship by Sir Walter Raleigh. Young Shakespeare couldn't have helped but be fired

Oh No! Not Romeo

up by the sight of England's finest sailing off to put one over the Spanish, French (or whoever).
Ben turns to face the ship and asks: Could this have been the location that inspired him to write the tragic love story of Antony and Cleopatra. Ant, a Roman ruler who left the bed of a beautiful Egyptian queen and took to the high seas to protect her against his own countrymen? A play that gave birth to the most famous lines in English literature?
CUE Dave. He bursts over to the side of the ship and belts out: The boy I love is out in the Galleon, etc. Blows kisses, throws petals,
MONEY SHOT: Close up on Ben. Left gobsmacked again, can't believe it, open mouthed etc. Chinese tourists looking puzzled, politely clapping, embarrassed.. Job done.

'Well, it's succinct, I'll give you that, Charlie,' Ben says.

'And as long as Jennings knows his cue, I won't have to go near him till we do it. I take it you're paying him well; can't imagine he's doing it to make amends or anything noble like that.'

'You leave me to worry about that, Ben. He'll be well rewarded, so will the others. I've got two of the waiters filming it on their cameras. The rawer it looks the better. That's why I don't want any rehearsals. And not a word to anyone. I haven't said anything to Sam, can't risk it slipping out. That's why I typed the script myself. It would only take one of my rivals to get wind and I'd be sunk. All you've to worry about is acting dumbstruck again, but don't overdo it Ben, son.'

He shakes Ben's hand with the solemnity of an admiral sending his captain off to war. He suppresses the urge to salute but swings crisply to his right and walks briskly down the stairs, noting that Sam's door is closed. He wasn't going to make a point of knocking after what Charlie had said about secrecy. Strange of Charlie to say that. He wondered if he suspected Sam of being a double agent. It would explain how Jennings' agent learned about the run in with the City trader.

Ben needed some thought-time. He bought a baguette from a takeout cafe opposite the office and headed for the river. Just before the Tower of London he turned into the memorial garden for merchant seaman killed in war and sought out an empty bench. One bite into his crusty BLT baguette his mobile rang, so it was a choked 'hello' he uttered when he heard Sam's husky voice.

'You all right, Ben?' she said. 'Don't tell me you've lost your voice arguing with Charlie. I thought you were going to make peace, see what he had to offer. He's been playing his cards close to his chest all day. I know he's been working on another video idea, and as I didn't hear any glasses hit the floor this time I reckoned you'd struck a deal.'

Ben was caught on the hop. He didn't want to lie to her. But with Charlie's warning ringing in his ear he didn't want to take any chances by letting her in on the plan. The BLT came to the rescue. That one bite didn't intend sinking without another burst for freedom, and made its case to be ejected with a choking cough.

When Ben finally stopped, it was with a staccato squeak he said 'Sorry.. Sam.. can't… talk..' The line went dead immediately.

Ben decided his lunch had caused enough damage, threw it in a litter bin and headed down to the cobbled stretch of the embankment. He was still trying to identify something buzzing in the back of his mind, not even sure if it was a good or bad something, just knew it was important.

It was that song. That's what it was. He remembered where he's heard the tune before.

His thoughts were interrupted by the megaphoned voice of a guide from a tourist boat which had slowed down close to the Tower... 'And if you look down at the waterline you will see the infamous Traitor's Gate,' he bellowed.

The next call Ben took was on Wednesday at noon. It was Charlie, the politician manner had gone, to be replaced by Sid James.

'Been trying to reach you all morning and most of yesterday, Ben, old son. You been arranging a wedding or something? Never known you to be so engaged. Haw- haw.

'Hope you haven't got cold feet. They'll be a bloody sight colder if you pull out now and I have to throw you in the river, haw-haw.'

'Been busy, Charlie,' Ben said truthfully. 'Been rehearsing my role for today, getting into character, doing a bit of research.' True to a point. 'I'll be there, don't you worry. Wouldn't miss it for the world.'

He wasn't so confident when he greeted the group of Chinese waiters posing as his tour party. In fact he was nervous. He felt inside his canvas sling bag, for the umpteenth time. Felt reassurance. Here we go, he muttered to himself.

As they walked along Bankside, Ben slipped into character. He limbered up his voice by gathering the group a safe distance from the Juliet balcony and gave a truncated version of the story. The group of twelve nodded appreciatively and some even turned and made comments in Chinese. Ben guessed it was the Mandarin equivalent of 'rhubarb, rhubarb.'

Right on 2pm, he stood with his back to the port side of the Golden Hind. The group gathered in a rough arc before him. Several had video cameras out, noticeably two on the wings who seemed to have started recording. There were several tourists milling around too, including two young men, one considerably larger than his rather fragile-looking companion. Both had cameras and were taking shots of each other posing against the river backdrop.

'Just gather round a little closer, please,' Ben began.

'This was a very special place in the life of young William Shakespeare. More than 400 years ago he opened the first Globe Theatre near this site. He was the toast of London. He was rich. He was famous. But his fame meant he could no longer walk the streets unnoticed. And so he would come down to this river on moonlit nights, between plays, dressed as a sailor to seek solitude and inspiration.

'The vista before you was the provider for his fertile imagination. On many a storm-tossed night he would look out to see the Queen's galleons sail to war. Their colours flying high on the mast; the crew fired with hatred for the Spaniard. The words of their boastful shanties drifting across the tide.

'This, Shakespeare scholars believe, was the inspiration for the Bard's tragedy, Antony and Cleopatra. Marc Antony, the Roman ruler who left the bed of beautiful Egyptian queen and sailed to war against his own countrymen to protect her.'

Ben turns sideways onto the boat and sweeps his arm as if heralding the fleet and adds gravely: 'A play that gave birth to the most famous lines of all: "Friends, Romans and countrymen lend me your ears..."'

With immaculate timing a flamboyant figure above him appears and is singing: *The boy I love is out in the galleon, the boy I love is looking now at me...*'

In a husky but unmistakably feminine voice.

Sam is beaming down at her audience, flicking the ends of her Cleopatra wig suggestively and fluttering the heavily kohled eyelashes. With her gold tunic and high strappy sandals she looks the image of the Queen of the Nile. As imagined by a soft porn producer.

The Chinese group, who hadn't been told what would happen have burst into life, thrilled at this unexpected treat, and are shouting for more.

'There he is, can't you see, waving his handkerchief,
As merry as a robin that sings on a ....'

She stops and looks at Ben. No reaction. He hasn't moved an eyelid. He just stares and she freezes. He reaches into his bag and slips the clasp from the coil of rubber inside, but still holding it together, not allowing it to spring open. In one deft movement he sweeps it from the bag, tossing it underhand high into the air, where it opens - a three-foot green rubber snake with a bulbous head and dangling fork tongue. For a split second, time stands still as the latex reptile slithers in a sinuous salsa. Then comes to land around Sam's neck. She falls backwards, flat on the deck, swearing like an East End docker.

Ben swings round to face the cameras and with a smug grin says: 'Kiss my Asp, Cleo.'

An hour later, Jeremy is sitting in front of his new laptop at the flat. 'Come on in lads, we're ready to go in five,' he shouts towards the kitchen.

Two figures emerge, clutching beer bottles, looking like old style trade union bosses who'd been locked in overnight pay negotiations. Ben Wyman and Dave Jennings had cemented their entente cordiale by emptying the newly stocked fridge of two six packs.

Peace moves started on Tuesday when Ben realised they'd both been taken for a ride. By Charlie, aided by Sam. Ben told Jennings about the new video being filmed the next day, correctly guessing his old enemy knew nothing about it

'The revelation came when I finally nailed where I'd heard the tune *The Boy I Love is up in the Gallery* before,' Ben had explained. 'Sam was humming it on the night she came to the flat, pretending to be concerned for me, claimed to know nothing about the new video.'

'Let me stop you there, Wyman,' Jennings had interrupted aggressively. 'Why should I care if they are shafting you?'

Ben explained that he'd been told by Charlie that Jennings would be playing the part of Cleopatra. He'd been used as bait to get Ben to take part, a chance to get even.

'He knew how to press all the right buttons,' Ben elaborated. 'Knew that I couldn't resist trying to get revenge for the balcony stunt. By the way, do you know who paid for that?'

Jennings frowned. 'The bloke who owned the house, of course. He told me what a pain the tours had become, explained what I had to do. What I didn't know was that it'd be you down there as the tour guide.'

'The man you met was Charlie,' Ben said. 'He set it up and paid the bill. After I'd told him about the complaints he went round to see the house owner and cooked up the whole thing, hoping to whip up a publicity blockbuster. Crafty sod had me believing that you'd dreamt up the balcony stunt after being tipped off by Sam about the angry house owner.'

Jennings's anger at being used had soon turned to

thoughts of revenge. He was prepared to accept the hand of his old enemy Ben, if it would mean using it to hoist Charlie by his own petard.

Ben assured him that it would, and he would have the pleasure of filming it, along with his flatmate Jeremy on the quayside, by the Golden Hind.

The results of their efforts were now running on the laptop. Jeremy sat back smugly as it rolled, knowing something they didn't, for once.

It was better than the Balcony video, more spectacular with Sam in Cleo gear and the Golden Hind looking glorious. The crowning glory was the scene of her falling backwards, clasping a rubber snake entwined around her throat and the cut to Ben for his one-liner. But the coup de gras came with a line of Egyptian hieroglyphics appearing teletext fashion at the bottom of the screen on the last frozen frame, followed by an English translation.

In case of snakebite, call Charlie and Sam at Shakespeare's tours. They suck.

9.
White Jacket

MARY stood as straight as her 73-year-old spine permitted at the top of the cathedral's 21 steps, staring down at the waiting hearse.

Behind her, four pall bearers were poised for the descent, confident that the tilt of the oak veneer coffin on their shoulders was held in check by their collective grip. But try as they may to stay poker-faced, the more observant in the crowd lining the route detected a hint of a smile creasing the corners of their mouths.

Mary turned her head to the left and nodded to the Valve Grinders' Silver Band who were in a semicircle, instruments to lips, their backs to the statue of Archangel Michael looming over a shackled Devil. To the art critics, it was Jacob Epstein's finest work, acclaimed for its powerful symbolism in a city which rose again after the destruction of Hitler's bombs. To the incumbent of the coffin, the statue had presented a daily opportunity for his favourite gag about the Devil's "athletic" proportions.

Labour warhorse Bill (never-was-a-William) Sheepshank took a short detour to the statue every morning on his walk to the town hall, hoping to encounter a lingering tourist.

'Not only is it an artistic masterpiece but it's a marvel of engineering,' he would begin, before describing how thirty hidden bolts supported the two figures suspended on the cathedral's red sandstone east wall. Then, with a suggestive twinkle in his eye, added, 'You'll notice the Devil is particularly well hung.'

He boasted that the punch line always got a laugh from Aussies and Americans, but to his dying day he never admitted to the coachloads of Japanese tourists he left bewildered.

Now, two weeks after that dying day, he would finally get the unstinting, thunderous round of applause he so desperately courted throughout his 20 years as council leader.

The silver band's opening bars had the crowd puzzled. The tune seemed familiar but too slow. One or two frowned like contestants in a name-the-intro quiz, mouthing 'it isn't, is it?'

A cluster of Bill's drinking mates, who'd missed the service thanks to a third round of pints and whisky chasers at Wetherspoons, ended all doubts by chorusing 'Come on baby, light my fire. Try to set the world on fi...yer.'

As the cheers and clapping erupted, the trombonists pointed their instruments skywards, the cue for the band to spread apart like the wings of the archangel behind them, revealing Bill Sheepshank's trademark white dinner jacket hanging from the Devil's big toe. The more obvious appendage being out of reach.

The raucous laughter almost drowned out the Dean's shriek. He'd been standing modestly in the shadows waiting to receive the praise of the Bishop for persuading him, against his better judgment, to allow a cathedral service for the Labour veteran, who'd often been quoted as saying his faith was in Socialism not the Church.

Those who rushed to the Dean's aid believing he was suffering a seizure would later tell the Bishop he fell to the ground sobbing 'What the hell next?'

Mary provided the answer. Confidently turning to face the Devil, she reached forward to unhook the jacket, then carefully folded it over her left forearm like a deferential waiter's towel and led the pall-bearers at a measured pace to the hearse. As the coffin was lowered, she spread the jacket across its lid, and for a reason she couldn't explain, even to herself, saluted.

The jacket had taken centre stage earlier in the service, held aloft by Mary from the pulpit as she gave one of the two eulogies. She had been Bill's secretary for all his tenure as council leader and was the closest to family he had after his wife died five years ago.

The jacket was synonymous with the star-struck old Leftie. It was his prop. Today it was Mary's too, enabling her to deliver a warm, mischievous and wholly misleading account of Bill, 'the character'.

The dry-eyed mourners were complicit in her deceit. They had already listened to the tribute to Bill's political acumen, nodding along in all the right places, without for a moment agreeing with a word of it.

Bill had arrived in local politics via the conventional route. Shop steward in a factory supplying the motor industry, in his case Clarke's Valve Grinding where he'd served his apprenticeship, and an offer to stand for a shoo-in Labour seat on the council from his party branch. After five years of unspectacular service as a ward councillor he was elected leader of the ruling Labour group largely because he'd upset the fewest number of his colleagues.

He was liked for his personal qualities but not respected as a leader. The jibe amongst his critics was that while his heart was in the right place, his mind wasn't. Nobody quite knew where it was. Nevertheless Bill's backside was invaluable. It was keeping the leader's seat warm for one of them.

Even his opponents on the Tory bench would concede that Bill was popular; a crowd pleaser with the common touch. He revelled in the limelight and the white jacket ensured he usually got it.

'Bill got his beloved jacket from a bingo-caller at Butlins in the summer of 1979,' Mary began her eulogy, holding it out at arm's length.

'He stood in for him when he took a funny turn during double jackpot night. Bill knew the ropes because he did the same job at the Grinders' club on the odd Saturday.

'He went down well on the bigger stage and believed it stemmed from the confidence he got from wearing the jacket, which he conveniently forgot to return.

'From then on, as many of you know, the jacket and

Bill were inseparable. You might say joined at the hip, but the material wouldn't quite stretch that far. Bill never managed to do up any of the buttons.'

Relieved at the opportunity to shake off their pretend serious faces, the mourners gave a hearty chuckle, some clapped. It was enough of a distraction for Mary to slip the jacket discreetly to one of the pall-bearers, whose temporarily idle hands would find light work with the Devil.

Over the next 15 minutes Mary recounted 'Bill and The Jacket's Best Bits,' starting, appropriately, with the time George Best came to the city to play in an exhibition game for charity. Bill's preparation to meet his soccer idol was extraordinary. He didn't shave for a week, hoping to affect a grizzled Besty look, albeit one five stones heavier, looking as if he had a football stuffed under his vest.

It didn't occur to Bill that the one-time fashion icon would be unimpressed by his white jacket with a cut-out number 7 stuck on the back. Neither did it bother him that he'd not been invited to the reception at the football club sponsoring Best's visit.

He blustered in carrying a white plastic football, signed by himself and the Lord Mayor that afternoon, and presented it to the speechless star as a 'Gift from the people of Coventry'.

The resulting Press picture was given joint top billing on Bill's trophy board back at his office, alongside the one of him and Muhammad Ali. The former world heavyweight champ had been on a publicity tour of the

UK, hooking up with all the British opponents he'd last seen flat on the canvas at his feet.

Jack Bodell, unflatteringly dubbed the Swadlincote Swine Herder, hadn't fought Ali but had been one of his sparring partners and now ran a chip shop in one of the tougher areas of the city. The potential for an easy headline hadn't escaped Ali's advisers. It was a gift for the Press.

Bodell and Ali were to be pictured at the fryer holding a bag of fish and chips between them with Ali's fist under Jack's lantern jaw. Ali-oop! Bodell takes a battering from the Greatest. Easy.

Bill wasn't to be denied a walk-on part however and convinced the photographers that he'd reffed a few amateur bouts in his white jacket, which he happened to be wearing.

So it was that picture editors across the Midlands got their shots of Bodell and Ali squaring up at the chippy with the unexpected addition of Bill out-hamming them both as a ring ref, straining to keep them apart.

Mary began the final part of her eulogy by saying that this very cathedral played a major role in one of Bill's proudest moments.

The audience held its breath. The Belinda Beluma affair had not been without casualties, however much deserved, and it would be a brave soul who aired the story in public, never mind at a funeral.

'Yoko Ono,' Mary said after a teasing pause. The collective held-breath whistled its release around the cathedral's bare stone walls.

'Bill was a great fan of the Beatles. He never got to meet them but he did get to see Yoko when she visited Coventry on the anniversary of the acorn planting.'

This was nearly 40 years after Yoko and Lennon, in their first public appearance together, buried Peace Acorns in lawn near the Chapel of Unity, enclosing them in a white circular bench where people could sit and watch them grow. The first visitors decided they would take them home to watch. They stole them. Within days the bench vanished too. A finger of suspicion pointed at one of the cathedral canons who'd questioned the couple's suitability to use sacred ground for a publicity stunt when they were living in sin. Others believed Lennon had the bench removed in a fit of pique. The Bishop said nothing in the hope that it would soon be all forgotten.

Certainly the canon's attitude was forgotten four decades on when the cathedral invited Yoko to the dedication of a new seat and two Japanese oak trees which were planted to celebrate a Peace Month.

She accepted. The heady days of John and Yoko were long gone and this time plans were laid to ensure a media scrum didn't overshadow the peace message. Children from local schools would help with the planting and after the dedication Yoko would have a brief walkabout among the public. Civic and church leaders would have to take a back seat

In the case of Bill, no seat at all. The Bishop and the Lord Mayor would do the formal meet and greet, he would have to take his place with the public on a taped-off stretch of lawn.

'Bill was disappointed but took his place with the ordinary people lined up to watch Yoko,' Mary continued. 'But of course he was wearing his distinctive white jacket, and for the first time, a matching pair of trousers.

'Those of you old enough to have bought The Beatles' Abbey Road album will know the Fab Four are pictured in line on a zebra crossing with Paul McCartney out of step, an omen of the group's impending split in Beatle folklore. John Lennon, supposedly the cause of the break-up, is leading the line, wearing a trademark white suit. When he planted the acorns in 1968 he was also wearing a white suit.

'Needless to say Bill's crafty tribute worked and he got his picture with Yoko when she returned that day.'

Mary didn't feel it was necessary to add that Bill schemed to be in exactly the right position. He had ordered Mary to 'borrow' a confidential plan of the proposed walkabout so he knew precisely where to place himself to be in Yoko's line of vision as she stepped out with the Bishop.

She finished her tribute with an enigmatic adaptation of the words of Lennon's most famous song.

'You may say Bill in his white jacket was a dreamer, but he was not the only one. I hope you'll join us at the reception at one where we can imagine more of his exploits.'

By 12.30 in the Events Lounge of the Valve Grinders' Club, inroads had already been made into the ham sandwiches and forays further down the buffet table had weakened the ranks of scotch eggs and sausage rolls.

The council's Press office team had made the strikes and was now attacking the beer supply, having been tipped off it was a free bar. The 30-minute start over the rest of the guests had meant forgoing the committal at the crem for the Jacket and Bill.

By the time the other mourners arrived at the club, communications officer Jon Vesty was fully charged for a melodramatic version of the story that Mary had left out her eulogy.

'It started with a leaked memo from the Chief Constable to his deputy saying Belinda Beluma was coming to Coventry Cathedral for the funeral of Jackie Felix, the animal rights campaigner,' he began.

'News spread like a spill of hot olive oil along the polished tiles of the town hall, flowed from the mayor's office along the wainscoted corridors to the councillors' meeting rooms and into our office where it dripped onto the worried brow of our line manager, Sylvia Slaughter.

'Sylvia's career survival depended on sensing a wobble to her daily tightrope act. This was a potential 10 on the Richter Scale.

'We minions were less finely tuned to the danger and the men whose pulses would have raced at the thought of seeing Belinda in the flesh no longer had pulses. They'd long gone.

'I remember thinking Old Watson, our previous boss, would be banging on his coffin-lid at missing this.'

'Was Belinda Beluma very famous, then?' interrupted

his junior colleague, Anastasia, who'd been with the department six months and whose celebrity history began with Lady Gaga.

'Sex siren actress of the late Fifties and Sixties,' Vesty responded tersely, as if it was common knowledge. He'd gone over the cuttings that morning to remind himself, hoping he'd get a chance to show off.

'Italian-French. Actress, pin-up, model. About 60 at the time we're talking about and living as a recluse in Corsica, where she ran an animal sanctuary. Her arrival in Cov would be the biggest thing since Godiva turned out without a vest.'

Had Sylvia Slaughter been at the wake, and not taking a swim at her retirement villa in Ibiza, she would have given a more prosaic account of her reaction to the news, which was: 'It's a bloody nightmare, that's what it is. Sheepshank will be dusting down his white jacket already.'

Her prediction was out by 20 minutes. The Jacket had already been taken from the locked mahogany wardrobe in Bill's office by Mary and released from its plastic sheath.

'Has this shrunk, Mary? Used to fit me like a glove.' The buttons were at full stretch but still failed to bridge Bill's ample beer gut.

'Needs a quick dry clean, too. Get one of the girls to take it, soon as.'

'Councillor Sheepshank,' Mary replied, in the sharp tone she used when he needed a reality check, 'the police chief has been on the phone again. He's insistent that no-one should approach Miss Beluma; she wants nothing to detract from the funeral service and intends to slip into the cathedral without fuss. She definitely doesn't want to meet dignitaries for a photo call.'

'Of course, of course, sensitive time, I realise that, Mary. I don't intend to bluster up to her as the hymns start and ask for an autograph.

'I shall be discretion itself, wait until she walks down the steps and introduce myself and offer to have Jason drive her back to the airport in the civic Jag.

'And I've just thought of a nice touch: red, white and blue ribbons on the Jag. It'll help lift the mood. Hands across the water, united in grief sort of thing. Do you think a black tie with the lucky white jacket sends out mixed messages?'

At that, Mary conceded the opening skirmish and conserved ammunition for the battle ahead. Besides, the danger was not to the sensitivities of a faded film siren. She must have endured far worse than a star-struck sweaty councillor embracing her. The threat lay much nearer. In fact, just next door at the mayor's office. For if there was a bigger ego feeding on reflected glory than Sheepshank it belonged to that year's first citizen, Lord Mayor William (never- call- me- Bill) Wolfe, solicitor and leader of the Tory group which had an outside chance of toppling Labour at the May local elections. A swing of six seats would see Wolfe taking over as council leader and, as Mary came with the job, she would then be his secretary.

She had spent the last ten years manipulating

Sheepshank, playing on his vanity, convincing him that his hold on the leadership was earned through his skill and diplomacy; most of all his knack of winning the electorate's hearts and minds.

Much as she detested it, the ridiculous white jacket played a leading role in Bill's act. Better another performance from the jacket if it could be arranged than see a vote-catching initiative grabbed by Wolfe. The prospect of starting again with that smarmy upstart as leader filled her with dread.

Although the offices of the council leader and Lord Mayor butted, not a peep could be overheard, however much Wolfe tried as he hovered by the party wall, pretending to be deep in reflection.

The thick sandstone walls of the town hall, built in the 1930s in a mock Gothic had withstood WW2 bombing.

So, too, had the walls of the medieval St Michael's cathedral. But Hitler's incendiary bombs had rained down on its roof, leaving it a gutted shell.

The Ruins, as they were known, stood alone in the post-war years, until 1962 when on an adjoining plot a new St Michael's Cathedral was consecrated.

The symbolic pairing of The Ruins alongside the modernist sister structure was hailed as a bold vision of hope for future world peace and reconciliation. But, to the cynics, they were also regarded as the city's USP for town-twinning, which kept the civic leaders in an abundance of 'goodwill' foreign visits.

Occasionally, though, even the fiercest critic would concede the Council and Church had their fingers on the

White Jacket

public pulse and could make an inspired decision.

Wolfe was quite happy to let the public think so.

For the time being, anyway. It was he who had planted the seed for the latest crowd pleaser and, when it came to fruition, he intended to reap the harvest of publicity.

The Bishop had agreed that the cathedral would host the funeral service of animal rights campaigner Jackie Felix, who had, died tragically trying to stop a lorry carrying baby lambs. The young mum lost her life slipping beneath the truck's wheels while picketing against the export of the animals. Her cause attracted a wave of support largely through her commitment and tenacity. She became a heroine in the eyes of animal lovers and the wider fringe of class warriors attracted by her crusade, The tragedy elevated her to international martyr when her picture alongside stock photos of caged lambs were shown worldwide.

She was also undeniably beautiful. A young Jane Fonda with a punk nose ring and army jacket. Thousands wanted to pay their respects by attending the funeral, including the movie sex goddess, Belinda Beluma, outspoken advocate of animal rights whose countrymen regarded pretty much any creature, apart from toy dogs, as fair game for the pot.

Mary had to act fast if she was to thwart Wolfe stealing the BB show. Bill Sheepshank might have the huff and puff but it was the Wolfe's guile that would bring her house down. She called Sylvia Slaughter.

Jon Vesty was also finding that huff and puff could only

take him so far. The truth was he only knew the bare bones of the story and hadn't been party to the plan cooked up by Mary and Sylvia.

He was floundering for facts and wasn't helped by Anastasia interrupting him again, asking if John Lennon was married to Beluma.

'No my dear, he wasn't.'

The answer came from Mary who'd been standing unnoticed for the last few minutes at the back of the Events Room, cringing at Vesty's colourful account.

'And I'm afraid I can't tell you everything that transpired between me and Sylvia, but let's say we recognised a common threat to both our careers if the two egos collided head on.

'An entente cordiale had to be formed, and with Sylvia's A-level French and my diploma in life we managed it. Or at least, we provided the platform.

'We couldn't have anticipated that one of the parties would plunge headlong off it.'

Mary's pledge of confidentiality was soon washed away by the free vodka and tonics passed to her by a relieved Vesty.

She revealed that Sylvia had flown to Corsica and driven to Beluma's enclave to plead their case, armed with a large bag of dog biscuits.

The actress was intrigued by the English woman who had turned up dressed for the beach clutching a sack of Waggy Wafers. It made a change from the usual bouquets of flowers sent by sly journalists working on stories of the 'reclusive' life they had invented for her.

Beluma's grasp of English was on a par with Sylvia's fingertip hold on French-Italian and nowhere near sufficient to understand the complexities of political rivalries in provincial England. But one of her staff was. Derek, unaffectionately, known as The English, a former police dog handler who looked after the strays taken in by Beluma. He'd been one himself, bumming around the Europe's beaches in a midlife crisis, when he'd washed up outside her compound looking for work. He understood perfectly the quandary that had brought Sylvia to Corsica. It was the sort of pathetic power struggle that had driven him out the police force in England.

As he translated the sorry tale to his employer, Sylvia opened the Waggy Wafers and started sharing them randomly to the pack of scraggy salivating mongrels circling at her feet.

Derek had to come to her rescue again as she disappeared under a mountain of shaggy coats and slobbering mouths. Much to the amusement of her host, whose image of English eccentricity was pleasingly confirmed.

The incident seemed to make Derek's pitch easier. Sylvia still couldn't keep up with the rapid fire exchanges but she could tell it was going well and joined in enthusiastically when Belinda laughed. She hadn't a clue what about.

When Sylvia left for the 4pm flight home, she was brimming with hope. 'Peace in our time,' was the simple text she'd earlier sent to Mary. Which was overstating it somewhat as she didn't even have a slip of paper from Beluma to wave as her ally greeted her at Birmingham Airport.

Over coffees – espresso for Sylvia, milky instant for Mary – she recounted the verbal deal she'd struck. Any formal greeting from the Lord Mayor or council leader was out of the question. She was to be left alone at the cathedral. Guaranteed. Or she would simply not come. And she would tell the English Press why.

'You can tell your Messieurs Wolfe and Sheepshank to put that in their pipes and smoke it,' was how Derek diplomatically translated it. For Sylvia understood exactly what she meant when she jabbed the air with her middle finger.

In exchange, Beluma agreed to meet the politicians at the airport where her Lear jet would be landing an hour before the funeral service. Wolfe and Sheepshank would be given five minutes to have a picture taken with her and she would tell them about her animal welfare sanctuary. Then they must leave.

'It wasn't a hard job to get Bill's agreement,' Mary told the growing audience at the club.

'He would get the picture he craved. The white jacket would win again. Beluma didn't want anything that smacked of an official ceremony so the civic Jags would stay in the garage and the Lord Mayor's chain of office remain in the safe.

'Bill was quick to realise he had no choice, anyway. He couldn't ambush BB at the cathedral now we had an agreed protocol.

'Wolfe, though, was furious. He had suggested using the cathedral and wanted full credit for it.

'Beluma's decision to attend was the icing on the cake, as far as he was concerned, and we were forcing him to hand a slice to a glutton in a white jacket.

'We'd underestimated his ambition. His self promotion wasn't aimed just at leading his party to victory in the council elections. His real goal was to catch the eye of his national party leaders for a fast-track to a winnable Parliamentary seat.

'He was convinced that personal publicity was the fuel that would power him through the ranks. Being pictured with a world famous star at the funeral of a local heroine would have put him firmly on the starting grid for Westminster. When Sylvia broke the news of the agreement to him his wheels fell off.'

Mary had often wondered why they hadn't realised then that he wouldn't take it lying down. In the following days he acted normally: bad tempered, sullen, and rude. So there was no reason to suspect he wasn't sincere when he finally said yes to the deal. There was one proviso. He couldn't bring himself to travel to the airport sharing a car with Sheepshank. It was a given that they wouldn't exchange a word, anyway, but he was damned if he'd allow the jacket to mock him en-route.

Having secured the promise of separate cars he carried on in his obnoxious manner, apparently resigned to his reduced role. In reality he was plotting to upstage Sheepshank and grab the spotlight back.

He needed a gimmick. Something, certainly not a bloody vulgar jacket, that would impress a woman who had seen and done most things in life while he was still waiting for a first kiss in the playground. A cute animal, with a back story of abuse, was an obvious choice for a gift. Too obvious though. It had backfire alert written all over it. He took to the internet for inspiration. Tapping Belinda's Desires into the search engine proved an eye-opener. It also brought a discrete visit from the council's Head of Computer Compliance, reminding him that his laptop was for authorised business use only.

In the end it was a combination of yesterday's technology and the net which gave Wolfe what he was looking for.

A retro gifts shop called Have A Nice Daze had opened in the south Leicestershire market town where he lived with his solicitor wife and their twin boys. They were studying law at Warwick Uni. Their ambition to be barristers started at nine, sparked by a family outing to the public gallery at the Old Bailey.

Wolfe had been intending to buy a quirky birthday card for the boys, who would be twenty in a fortnight. As agreed in the Family Contract he had drafted when they had finished A-Levels, their birthday present would be 25 per cent towards their Student Loans each year until they were 21 or had graduated, whichever was the sooner.

A not insignificant sum and Wolfe felt it did no harm to remind them of their parents' sacrifice by halving the birthday card budget. They would be receiving just one between them this year.

Have a Nice Daze was actually two shops. A section was rented out to a retired electronics engineer who renovated old Bakelite radios and Dansette record players, trendy sought-afters in circles where dinner parties still survived.

A few were displayed in the window which Wolfe had his nose pressed against. But it wasn't those that caught his eye. He had zoomed in on a chic transistor radio which had "Sixties" written all over it. Too stylish to be English. Finished in black faux leather with chrome trim. Shaped like a Paris courtesan's clutch bag. It had to be Italian or French.

The abbreviations on the tuning dial gave Wolfe hope. FR1, EUR, MON, LUX. Had he been wearing his glasses he would have saved himself further anxiety, for it had "Made in France" running vertically along the fascia.

Wolfe was delighted to find the radio. His hands were trembling when he came to pay the £70 tag.

His pulse had been in overdrive since he'd Googled Optalix, the manufacturer's name. Among the jungle of images that filled his screen was one of a saucy poster featuring a come-hither blonde taking a soapy bath, in apparent ecstasy at listening to the Optalix radio perched next to the soap dish.

To Wolfe's by then unstable mind it was a young Belinda, probably between sexpot movies earning a Riviera villa with a lucrative modelling assignment.

He would have the poster copied, printed and framed to match the dimensions of the radio. They would be wrapped together modestly in plain brown paper to fit snugly into the pocket of his black crombie which he'd be wearing to the funeral.

By then the pocket would be empty. He would have taken the gift out for Belinda after kissing her on both cheeks – clinically practised with a reluctant Mrs Wolfe over the preceding days – humbly proffering "Un petit cadeau from a bewitched schoolboy who dreamed that one day he'd meet you."

He'd have practised that too, in French. But not with Mrs Wolfe, who would be complaining her cheeks were chapped through constant wiping.

'Take that, Mr White Jacket Sheepshank,' he murmured to himself as he visualised Belinda teary-eyed with gratitude, the radio clasped to her chest and his arms enveloping her as a long-lost lover's might, ruing the years they'd spent apart.

'We knew nothing of Wolfe's surprise package when we set off for the airport,' Mary said. She had the attention of a full house now.

'I led the way, driving Bill, white jacketed, naturally, in the passenger seat of my Focus. Sylvia was right behind in a VW hatchback with the windows open to counter the whiff of an overheated Wolfe sweating beneath a heavy crombie.

'We allowed plenty of time for the 10-mile journey and expected to be at the airport well before the 10am landing.

'Then we hit a traffic jam two miles short of the airport. At 10.15 we were headed for the VIP arrivals pickup area when Sylvia's VW roared past with four hands on the steering wheel and Wolfe's manic red face pressed against the windscreen, forcing me to swerve into a skid that spun the car 180 degrees, leaving us facing the way we'd come. The tyres were shredded.

What transpired formed the nub of a report by the Airport Intelligence Special Branch officers investigating potential terrorist threats. Holidaymakers arriving for flights to the sun gave statements describing a rotund middle-aged man in a white jacket leaping out of the stricken Focus shouting 'Bloody Hell, it's them' at a white limousine pulling out of a barrier-controlled service road.

White Jacket man showed surprising agility for a man of his build, they said, vaulting the rails of the short-stay car park and running off towards the south-bound exit gate, A short cut which would have seen him head off the limo, had he been running at 60mph. But estimates put his pace at no more than 3 mph.

How he managed to get there in time was explained by a party of Italian businessmen who'd flown to Birmingham to watch rugby international and were waiting for a coach outside VIP Arrival. Their statement confirmed a VW being driven at reckless speed, with a man and woman fighting over the wheel. The vehicle executed a u-turn and took out their line of baggage trolleys. They saw it roaring off in hot pursuit of a white limousine.

They were amazed to see the chauffeur of the limo slow up, waiting for the VW to reach his rear end, then slamming on his brakes. His reinforced bumper easily took out the VW's radiator.

He'd told the investigators he'd dealt with enough crazy paparazzi down the years of driving Mme Beluma to see off a couple of amateurs trying their luck. Still, he added, he had to smile when in his rear view mirror he saw a furious woman waving a buckled chrome grille at a fleeing red-faced man in a black coat.

Satisfied that he was out of zoom lens distance, he pulled up to check for any damage, couldn't find a scratch, and before driving off lowered the internal glass partition and assured the three occupants, Belinda and two bodyguards, that all was okay.

'Things were far from okay,' Mary said, shaking her head sadly. Vesty immediately handed her a glass of vodka unsullied by tonic.

'The chauffeur's actions gave Bill enough time to get in position...right in the middle of the south bound exit road.

'I'll give him his due, he was absolutely fearless; standing ramrod straight, chest full out, almost in line with his belly, right arm fully extended and palm cocked at the oncoming traffic. Stop!

'I can think of only two other hand signs more universally understood than Bill's signal. Any British driver would have chosen the two-fingered one to respond to a fat bloke standing in the road wearing a white jacket.

'But the French chauffeur was accustomed to traffic police in Monte Carlo dressed in white directing traffic.

'He instinctively slowed when he saw the white jacketed figure ahead signalling him to halt, stopped 30 yards short, bemused at the sight of the man beaming at him. He had never seen a smiling traffic cop and was beginning to have his doubts about pulling up when the figure boomed: "Je Suis Bill Sheepshank. Vous avez Miss Beluma, Sill-vous-plate?"

'I'd arrived on the scene by then,' Mary continued. 'Just in time to hear three voices inside the limo shout in unison "Merde!"

'Bill took it to mean welcome. He hit the ground grovelling, kissing both Beluma's hands as he knelt before her like an unworthy subject, then springing up to kiss the chauffeur on the cheeks.

'The bodyguards didn't escape Bill's charm blitzkrieg and seemed genuinely impressed when he flourished snapshots of himself alongside George Best, Ali and Yoko Ono.

'Belinda relaxed and began telling Bill about her animal sanctuary. Seizing his chance, the old fox pulled out his pocket camera and handed it to his new bodyguard mates, indicating they take a shot of him with the actress.

'When Bill grabbed Belinda's waist in a bear-hug I thought at first the high scream was hers. Then came the terrifying realisation of its origin when it was followed by: "Belinda, stand clear, don't do it. I am the one you should be with."

'Charging down the carriageway came Wolfe in his crombie, waving a suspicious-looking brown package in the air.

'The smaller of the bodyguards was first to react,

hurling himself at Wolfe's tiring legs, felling him like an axe would a sapling

'His fellow guard weighed in like a mauling rugby forward, wrenching back Wolfe's shoulders, forcing the release of the package trapped beneath him.

'Once he'd got a clear sight of it he gradually edged it out with his toe and shouted for the chauffeur to come close. Still crouched down, he scooped it up with both hands and threw it backwards between his own legs. The chauffeur took the catch with the confidence of rugby pro, and ran for the fire emergency water reservoir. He never made it. The group of angry Italians who just had their luggage smashed were looking for a scapegoat and brought him down five yards short with a series of bone-crunching tackles.

'The chauffeur's cries of "bomb" were ignored as they ripped open the package to reveal a radio and picture bound together. The fact that he was French and clearly a rugby player sealed his fate.

'He was dragged to the edge of the reservoir bent over with the radio placed carefully between his buttocks. The Italians chose their least skilful player to take the conversion. It took him three goes before he managed to kick the radio cleanly into the water.'

There was complete silence in the club as the mourners struggled to take in the image. Some of the men robbed their backsides, others recovered more quickly and stared at Mary in anticipation.

'William Wolfe was arrested on suspicion of dangerous driving, stalking and endangering public safety. No charges were made after medical examinations found him mentally unfit to plead.

But it finished his marriage and his solicitor's practice. Wolfe's political ambitions were dead in the water, along with the transistor radio, which spent two days on the bottom of the reservoir before being recovered.

He was able to claim his pension early on medical grounds and sell his practice, leaving him enough after the divorce settlement to retire to Dorset where he is now a volunteer at a donkey sanctuary.

'The unfortunate chauffeur took his time in recovering from his bruising encounter but was helped by the balm of 10,000 Euros from the deeply apologetic Italians.'

Anastasia, wary of being chastised for interrupting again, put her hand in the air, caught Mary's eye and posed the questions on everyone's lips.

'So, I suppose Miss Beluma flew straight back to Corsica and Bill Sheepshank never got his picture? What a shame, he seemed such a nice man.'

Mary smiled enigmatically, weighing up her response.

'You're mistaken on two counts, dear. 'But on this occasion, two wrongs might make you a right, about Bill. I'll leave that for you to decide.

'Belinda Beluma and her bodyguards didn't fly home until later that day. They stuck to the plan and slipped into the cathedral as the service began, having been dropped off in a quiet corner of the town hall car park.

They were leaving by the same route when BB lifted her veil and was recognised by a sharp-eyed reporter.'

Bill had kept his side of the bargain by staying silent

about BB's presence during the day and even when the story broke refused to comment or claim credit.

'Until now, Mary announced solemnly.

'He left instructions in his will that I should show you all today one of his most treasured possessions.' She strode over to the club notice board and lifted a shroud of black cloth which everyone had assumed was there in deference to Bill's passing, screening announcements of bingo nights.

It was more a last hurrah to the old devil: a poster-sized photograph taken through the limo's wound-down window. Bill beaming at the camera from the driver's seat, chauffeur's cap perched jauntily on his head, one arm on the steering wheel and his other hugging a bemused Belinda Beluma into the folds of his white jacket.

'Nice of him to chauffeur them to the cathedral. Wasn't it?' Mary asked.

'Even nicer if he'd taken me as well but he drove off while I was still on the grass verge putting the camera away.'

10.
When Blue turns to Grey

HILARY was on the phone again last night, still banging on about something to do with a glut of books about boy wizards, whips and chains.

'Thank god there are still old stagers around like you, Benno, observing real life from behind a cream scone at Betty's tea shop,' she said. By way of a compliment. I suppose.

Naturally, I felt obliged to mutter something in return about her own expertise (a knack of winning prestigious literary prizes, if I'd been honest) based entirely on my reading of barely a couple of pages of her latest winner before falling asleep in Camden Library one wet Wednesday afternoon.

Her rant had pointed me again to the nagging thought I may have been a little high-minded in refusing to read a line of Harry Potter and his wandering wand and fetish for ironwork.

It was after leaving the library and cycling shakily towards Waterstones that I first spotted the queue of women snaking from the shop, halfway up the street. Others were striding out of the doorway victoriously clutching books tightly to heaving bosoms, pointedly turned away from the grasping hands of the waiting throng.

'Fifty Shags a Day,' my publisher explained that afternoon.

'Bloody phenomenon, new genre. Mummy porn, atrociously written but making an absolute bloody mint, Benno dear.'

The seed was planted, so to speak, there and then. And fertilised the next day when news broke that JR Ewing, creator of the boy Potter was outed as a closet crime writer. And, infuriatingly, now a bestseller in that as well.

If she can do it, I reasoned to myself and later my publisher, a 'National Treasure' like yours truly – whose personal treasure wouldn't fill a pirate's pocket – could stoop to a bit of down and dirty if there was filthy lucre to sweep up. Under a pseudonym, naturally.

And so Dalton Montana was created, writer and leading man of the bonkbuster for porn-again grannies.

Turned out my publisher had got the title wrong earlier. He meant Fifty Shades of Grey but his imagination got the better of him. So ageing bachelor Montana's diary-style book would be a lumpy-bits-and-all riposte: Fifty Coats of Magnolia.

In my mind's ear I could hear that rather droll gardener Alan Titchmarsh, who some say does sound like me, reading it out in a wistful monologue for Book At Bedtime on Radio Four.

Or perhaps the rotund northern comedian Peter Kay would give it a shot, add a bit of bottom to the listeners' picture of Dalton Montana.

To get myself off on a sure footing I decided the first chapter would be based on a real-life incident, with a licence to kerb-crawl along the gutter of my imagination for embellishment.

And so the action started with a steamy scene in my, that is Dalton's, front room while decorating, wearing just starched white dungarees – the sort with a bib and no sleeves – and a dab of turps behind each ear. Pots of sexual imagery. "Undercoats of sensuality," as my publisher's blurb put it. "Peeling back the layers of domestic drabness to expose the naked plaster and reveal the virgin wood that has lain beneath Matt Emulsion for too long."

By the by, what's Matt Emulsion ever done to bring a bit of sparkle to the bedroom? He sounds like the dullard you'd avoid in a pub, forever moaning on about how with the right teachers he could have been an eggshell finish, gone to college even and got his Satin. But he was never given the chance to shine.

In the opening passage, I'm dipping my inch-flat brush in Geisha's Flush, satin sheen finish. I was torn between that and Desert Whisper or Harlot's Hint in soft velvet. Magnolia to you and me. Or three shades of eye wash at

£40 a tin.

Geisha's Flush, a hint of the Orient, exotic, mysterious. Oozing with Eastern Promise. Why is she flushed? Probably from the embarrassment of charging 40 quid a time for her paint.

Anyway, back to the plot. I've got a seven-foot strip of lining paper on the trestle table, dripping with Solvite heavy-duty paste, sprinkled with a dash of Old Spice aftershave leftover from Christmas 1983, when the home help, Mrs Jarvis bursts in, alerted by my cry of 'We've won the EuroLottery!'

I'd carefully chosen my moment, knowing that she would be taking her post-polishing shower and nothing less than the thought of a half share of Euro squillions would bring her rushing downstairs in a state of undress.

Before you could say 'Roll Over' I'd whipped the lining paper round her from neck to toe; wrapping her up like an Egyptian mummy, unable to move a muscle.

I could tell she was instantly locked in a prison of passion because her eyelids were drooping, she was breathing hard and had ripened as red as a tomato on heat.

I didn't hold back. With cold deliberate strokes I ran the freshly-dipped paint roller along her prostrate figure. Up those bound legs, held together like a mermaid's tail, across the swell of her buttocks rising like two medicine balls under house arrest, and along the arch of her shuddering back.

Her muffled sobs were broken with gasps of 'Please,

please... don't. Stop!'

But I was on a delirious roll, hearing only 'don't stop', frantically working on getting a smooth finish, leaving no patches, blissfully running the sheep's wool roller around those undulating papered curves, cornering tantalisingly along hill and down vale.

With Mrs Jarvis beyond speech and gripping the table edge as if her life depended on it, while I brandished the roller like a demonic conductor of sin, it was a struggle to turn her over. In a moment of inspired eroticism I managed to splash an extra dollop of paste beneath her considerable frontage and used the roller to flip her over like a wet chub on a fishmonger's slab.

I was bending down for my inch-flat brush to finish the nooks and crannies when the paper split and her arms burst free.

With an ear-splitting cry and a dungaree-splitting thrust she grabbed the roller and rammed it at me like an exocet. Into an orifice that dare not speak its name.

Had it not been freshly dipped in Geisha's Flush no doubt the pain would have been more excruciating, my cry more blood-curdling.

But there was no time for such thoughts then. The pasteboard came crashing down on my head followed by Mrs Jarvis, screaming like a paper-mache she-wolf and intent on forcing a plastic bucket down my throat.

Before I passed out, I remember groaning, 'How was it for you?'

*Epilogue. A messy business with Mrs Jarvis in all senses. She finally settled out of court for a sum that ensures I won't make a bean from the book.

More worryingly, a sly diary piece has appeared in Telegraph under the heading 'Benno Du Jour' hinting that I am writing a 'sexed up' account of a misspent youth, lying beneath the soft underbelly of sin that was Harrogate in the 1950s.

Publisher denies being the source of a leaked teaser to ratchet up interest but makes a Freudian slip when gleefully announcing offers for serialisation rights are "already on the paste table from the Sunday Times and Nuts."

Author's Note

The fact is.... All these stories are fictional. Most self-evidently so. But some contain elements of historical fact which should be acknowledged.

In a footnote to the first story, Walking Keef's Dog, I have elaborated on where fact stops and fiction begins. The Stones did play two shows at the Coventry Theatre on March 6, 1971, and Keith Richards arrived clutching his pet spaniel, Boogie. But sadly Boogie didn't escape. I took him on a flight of fantasy.

While all the characters and plots in White Jacket are entirely fictional, most of the cited examples of celebrity visits to Coventry happened. John Lennon and Yoko Ono planted acorns as a peace gesture in the grounds of the city's cathedral in June 1968. Yoko returned for a ceremony to honour that event in October 2005. Muhammed Ali came to the city in August 1983 and was met by his old sparring partner and former British heavyweight champ Jack Bodell who owned a chip shop. George Best visited Coventry many times after his playing days were over with Manchester Utd. The character of Belinda Beluma is made up but the idea of her visit to the cathedral funeral service has a parallel with the attendance of Brigitte Bardot to the city in honour of an animal rights activist killed in an accident while trying to prevent the export of young calves. The actress's appearance in February 1995 was discreet and dignified, and went unnoticed until she left.

All the characters and situations in Pinky and Perky are, like the old TV string puppets themselves, unreal if still a little disturbing. As far as I know, there is no widespread problem of impotency among folk fans, and they may feel (with some justification) they are victims of below-the-belt comedy. But hey, ho (and a nonny no) I shall to the Warwick Folk Festival go, in late July, for it does exist and has done so since 1979. There may well be Morris groups in blackface performing, but Benny and his Stickers will not be among them.

Neither will Oscar Wilde and Jim Morrison be caught in the act at Père Lachaise cemetery, for the undeniable reason that both are long dead. Their graves can be visited by the public along with those of the other celebrities mentioned. There is of course no old metro line in a corner of Gare Du Nord to magically whisk them there. Perhaps the most bizarre aspect of The Ballad of Jim and Oscar is what is true. In 1961 the reportedly large testicles of the winged messenger carved on Wilde's tomb were hacked off, never to be seen again, although it was rumoured a cemetery official had them as paperweights. Queen Elizabeth I (She's a Killer… Queen) stayed at Kenilworth Castle for nearly three weeks in 1575 as the guest of Robert Dudley who put of a lavish show, a gesture widely interpreted as a last ditch attempt by Dudley to win her hand. If that was the aim it didn't work. Recently there has been conjecture that Elizabeth had no desire to share her bed or power with any man. She was more attracted to her own sex. A reasonable theory given the example her father set for the male species, having got through six wives, with two beheaded. One of whom was Elizabeth's mother.

The characters and the plot in Boys are Back in Town are fictional but sprang from a real incident witnessed on the way to watch West Brom play Crystal Palace in a Premiership league game. The tram was suffocatingly overcrowded and a group of middle-aged away fans gave a performance of shameful boorishness, intimidating two teenage girls young enough to be their daughters. They happened to be Palace fans but it could have been any club, sadly. The remainder of the story is entirely fictional, apart from the result of the match, that is. Palace were hammered.

You Better, You Bet is not aimed at any one PFI hospital but is intended as a spoof on an 'initiative' that provides a huge cash cow for others to milk. In reality, no laughing matter. In 2015 the Daily Telegraph reported the NHS was spending more than £3,700 every minute to pay for privately financed hospitals. Or £2 billion a year. The cash is paid to private companies as part of an annual repayment fee for building and operating new hospitals as well as redeveloping old ones.

The remaining stories are sufficiently far-fetched to be in no danger of being mistaken for anything other than comic fantasy. I hope.

If there is a Benno (When Blue turns to Grey) out there trying to sell his paste-table, it's all a terrible coincidence. Sorry!

Steve Chilton is an award-winning newspaper journalist who worked for UK regional and national titles for more than 25 years.

He was born in Coventry midway between cathedrals. That is, after the destruction of the medieval St Michael's in 1940 and before the consecration of its replacement in 1962.

He still lives in the city with his wife, and clings to the hope that one day civic planners will get something right. This is his first collection of fiction, despite groundless accusations to the contrary.

The companion website for this book can be found at:

www.redbutton2.com

Lightning Source UK Ltd.
Milton Keynes UK
UKHW020633290419
341788UK00015B/1138/P